The PMS Murder

Books by Laura Levine

THIS PEN FOR HIRE

LAST WRITES

KILLER BLONDE

SHOES TO DIE FOR

THE PMS MURDER

Published by Kensington Publishing Corporation

A JAINE AUSTEN MYSTERY

The PMS Murder

LAURA LEVINE

KENSINGTON BOOKS
www.kensingtonbooks.com

For Michael, Barbara, Josh, and Ben

Acknowledgments

Many thanks, as always, to my editor John Scognamiglio and my agent Evan Marshall for their invaluable guidance and support. Thanks also to Joanne Fluke for her many acts of kindness and generosity, and to my friends and family for putting up with me while I'm writing. Thanks to Hiro Kimura for his snazzy cover, and to my feline technical advisor, my cat, Mr. Guy. (If I don't mention him somewhere in the acknowledgments, he's impossible to live with.) A special thanks to the readers who have taken the time to write me and visit me at my book signings. And finally—for loyalty and devotion above and beyond the call of duty—thanks to my number one fan and best friend, my husband, Mark.

Chapter 1

What's more painful than a mammogram? More excruciating than a bikini wax? More humiliating than spinach stuck to your front tooth?

Shopping for a bathing suit, of course.

There's nothing worse. Not even a root canal. (Unless it's a root canal in a bathing suit with spinach stuck to your front tooth.)

That's what I was doing the day I first became involved in what eventually became known as the PMS Murder: trying on a bathing suit. For some ridiculous reason I'd decided to take up water aerobics. Actually, for two ridiculous reasons: my thighs. Before my horrified eyes, they were rapidly turning into Ramada Inns for cellulite.

So I figured I'd join a gym, and after a few weeks of sloshing around in the pool, I'd have the toned and silky thighs of my dreams. But before I could get toned and silky, there was just one tiny obstacle in my way: I needed to buy the aforementioned bathing suit.

I knew it would be bad. The last time I'd gone bathing suit shopping, I came home and spent the night crying on the shoulders of my good buddy Jose Cuervo. But I never dreamed it would be this bad.

For starters, I made the mistake of going to a discount clothing store called the Bargain Barn. My checkbook was going through a particularly anemic phase at the time, and I'd heard about what great prices this place had.

What I hadn't heard, however, was that there were no private dressing rooms at the Bargain Barn. That's right. Everyone, I saw to my dismay, had to change in one ghastly mirror-lined communal dressing room, under the pitiless glare of fluorescent lights, where every cellulite bump looked like a crater in the Grand Canyon.

It's bad enough having to look at your body flaws in a private dressing room, but to have them exposed in a roomful of other women—I still shudder at the memory.

Making matters worse was the fact that I was surrounded by skinny young things easing their washboard tummies into size twos and fours. I once read that sixty percent of American women are a size twelve or larger. Those sixty percent obviously didn't shop at the Bargain Barn. But I shouldn't have been surprised. After all, this was L.A., the liposuction capital of the world, where it's practically against the law to wear a size twelve or larger.

I grabbed a handful of bathing suits, ignoring the bikinis and mini-thongs in favor of the more matronly models with built-in bras and enough industrial-strength spandex to rein in a herd of cattle.

I jammed my body into one hideous swimsuit after another, wondering what had ever possessed me to come up with this insane water aerobics idea. I tried on striped suits and florals; tankinis and skirtinis; blousons and sarongs. No matter what the style, the end result was always the same: I looked like crap.

One suit promised it would take inches of ugly flab from my waist. And indeed it did. Trouble was, it shoved that ugly flab right down to my hips, which had all the flab they needed, thank you very much.

I'd just tried on the last of the bathing suits, a striped tankini that made me look like a pregnant convict, when suddenly I heard someone moaning in dismay.

I looked over and saw a plump thirtysomething woman struggling into a pair of spandex bike shorts and matching halter top. At last. Someone with actual hips and thighs and tummy. One of the sixty percenters!

She surveyed herself in the mirror and sighed, her cheeks flushed from the exertion of tugging on all that spandex.

"My God," she sighed. "I look like the Pillsbury Doughboy with cleavage."

"Tell me about it," I said. "I look like the doughboy with cleavage, retaining water."

"Oh, yeah?" she countered. "I look like the doughboy with cleavage, retaining water on a bad hair day."

She ran her fingers through her blunt-cut hair and grimaced.

"Would you believe this is a size large?" she said, tugging at the shorts. "Who is this large on? Barbie?"

"Well, I've had it." I wriggled out of the tankini and started to get dressed. "I'm outta here."

I'd long since given up my insane water aerobics idea. No. I'd take up something far less humiliating. Like walking. And the first place I intended to walk to was Ben & Jerry's for a restorative dose of Chunky Monkey.

"I'm going to drown my sorrows in ice cream."

"Great idea," said my fellow sufferer. "Mind if I join you?"

"Be my guest."

And so, ten minutes later, we were sitting across from each other at Ben & Jerry's slurping Chunky Monkey ice cream cones.

"I'm Pam, by the way," my companion said, licking some ice cream from where it had dribbled onto her wrist. "Pam Kenton."

It was nice being with someone who ate with gusto. My

best friend Kandi has the appetite of a gnat and usually shoots me disapproving looks when I order anything more fattening than a celery stick. I know it's only because she cares about me and wants me to be one of the skinny forty percenters, but still, it can get pretty annoying.

"Actually," Pam said, "my last name isn't really Kenton. It's Koskovolis. Kenton is my stage name. I'm an actress. Of course, you know what that means in this town."

"Waitress?"

"You got it," she nodded. "And you?"

"I'm a writer."

"Really?" Her eyes widened, impressed. People are always impressed when I tell them I'm a writer. "What do you write?"

"Oh, industrial brochures. Resumes. Stuff like that."

Here's where they usually stop being impressed. Most folks find resumes and industrial brochures a bit of a yawn.

But Pam sat up, interested.

"You write resumes? I sure could use some help with mine. I'm getting tired of waitressing. I want a job where I get to sit down for a while."

"I'd be happy to help you with your resume," I offered.

A worry line marred her brow. "I couldn't afford to pay you much."

"Oh, don't worry about the money. I won't charge you."

Inwardly, I kicked myself. What was wrong with me? Why was I always giving away my services? If I started charging people, maybe I wouldn't have to shop at joints like the Bargain Barn. Oh, well. Pam seemed awfully nice, and it wasn't as if I had a lot of assignments that she'd be interfering with. In fact, my work schedule was scarily light.

"That's so sweet of you," Pam said. "How about I fix you dinner as payment?"

"Sounds great. When do you want to get together?"

"As soon as you can."

"How about tomorrow night?"

"Oh, I can't tomorrow," she said. "That's PMS night."

"PMS night?"

"A group of friends get together once a week to bitch and moan over guacamole and margaritas. We call ourselves the PMS Club."

"Sounds like fun."

"Hey, wait. I've got a great idea. Why don't you come with me? We're short on members right now and I think you'd be a great addition to the club. We could have dinner first at my place while we work on my resume and then head over to the club afterward. What do you say?"

"Are you sure the others won't mind?"

"No. They're going to love you; I'm sure of it. And it's really worthwhile. You get to share your innermost thoughts with like-minded women in a warm, supportive environment.

"Plus," she added, with a grin, "you get great guacamole and free margaritas."

"Sure," I said, never one to pass up a free margarita. "Why not?"

I was soon to find out exactly why not, but that's a whole other story. Stick around, and I'll tell it to you.

Chapter 2

I guess you could say the whole PMS mess was Kandi's fault. If she hadn't gone and gotten herself engaged, I never would've joined the PMS Club in the first place.

Yes, after years of dating some of the wartiest frogs on the planet, my best friend and constant dinner companion, Kandi Tobolowski, had done the unthinkable and finally met a prince. Of all places, in traffic school. They locked eyeballs over a lecture on Illegal U-turns and by the time they got to Lane Changing, Kandi knew she'd found the man of her dreams.

In the past, Kandi's dream men have invariably turned out to be nightmares. Last year, for example, she was madly in love with a performance artist, a guy whose act consisted of lying on stage in a vat of hot fudge sauce and spraying himself with Reddi-wip. Everything was rosy until she showed up at his loft one night and caught him in bed with another woman, a vibrator, and a jar of maraschino cherries.

But this time, it looked like she'd landed herself a winner. Her fiancé, Steve, was a true sweetheart, an attorney who worked pro bono for poor people. As far as attorneys went, he was a pussycat among piranhas.

I should have been happy for Kandi. And I was. Really. It's just that I couldn't help feeling a tad abandoned. I hardly ever saw her for dinner any more, and when I did Steve usually came with us. By the end of the evening I could practically feel them fondling each other's thighs under the table, putting me very much in the Fifth Wheel category. Which is why I was pleased and happily surprised earlier that day when Kandi called and asked me to have dinner, just the two of us. It would be nice, I thought, to have her all to myself for a change.

Back home, I found my cat Prozac asleep on the sofa, in the exact same position I'd left her six hours ago. Sometimes I think that cat was a statue in a former life.

"Hi, pumpkin. I'm home!"

The little darling jumped off the sofa and came racing to my side, rubbing my ankles with vibrating purrs of love.

Okay, so she didn't really do that. She pried open one eye, yawned a yawn the size of the Grand Canyon, then rolled over and went back to sleep.

But a cat owner can dream, can't she?

By now, I was regretting that scoop of Chunky Monkey I'd packed away at Ben & Jerry's. (Okay, two scoops.) So I headed to the bedroom and slipped out of my jeans and into a pair of elastic-waist pants. I was just breathing a sigh of relief when the phone rang.

A no-nonsense male voice came on the line. "Andrew Ferguson here. From Union National Bank."

Oh, darn. I couldn't possibly be overdrawn again, could I? Why, I just deposited a check last week. Or was it two weeks ago? I couldn't have run through all my money already. And even if I had, the bank had a hell of a lot of nerve calling me at home and invading my privacy. Wasn't it bad enough they socked me with a service charge every time I blinked an eye? I don't mind admitting I was pretty steamed.

"Look, here, Mr. Ferguson. Is it always your policy to call people at home like this?"

"I guess I could've e-mailed you, but I wanted to get in touch with you as soon as possible."

"If I'm overdrawn, I assure you the matter will be taken care of right away. I don't need a personal reminder."

"You don't understand—"

"When I've got scads of money in the bank, I don't see you calling me and thanking me, do I?"

There was a pause on the line.

"Ms. Austen, I'm not calling about your checking account."

"You're not?"

"No, I'm calling about the ad you answered in the *L.A. Times*. For someone to write our bank newsletter."

I'd answered that ad weeks ago and forgotten all about it. Here the man was calling me about a paying job, and the first thing I did was yell at him. Talk about your disastrous first impressions. I wouldn't be surprised if he hung up right then and there. But miraculously, he didn't.

"So do you think you can come in for an interview?" he asked.

"Of course."

"Wednesday morning at ten? Our downtown branch?"

"Absolutely! I'll be there. And I'm sorry about that checking account thing."

"That's okay. I'll be sure to have someone call you to thank you, though, the next time you've got scads of money in the bank."

I hung up and groaned. What an idiot I'd been. I couldn't believe he was still letting me come in for the interview. At least he seemed to have a sense of humor.

"Guess what, dollface?" I said, scratching Prozac behind her ears. "Mommy's got a job interview. Isn't that super?"

Whatever. Now scratch my back.

Ever her obedient servant, I scratched Prozac's back and then spent the next hour at the computer doing some research on Union National Bank. After my less than auspicious start, I wanted to be as knowledgeable as possible for my interview. I worked at it steadily, with just a tiny break for a quick game of computer solitaire (okay, five games of solitaire), until I heard the sweet sounds of Prozac yowling for her dinner.

I got up and went to the kitchen cupboard, where I took out a can of the diet cat food my vet had recommended on our last visit. I'd been meaning to give it to Prozac for the past several days, but I'd kept putting it off, afraid of the battle that might await me. After all, this was a cat that was used to Jumbo Jacks and the Colonel's chicken. Extra crispy, if you please.

But I'd promised the vet I'd give it a try, and now, I decided, was as good a time as any. I opened the can and poured the contents into Prozac's bowl.

"Here you go, sweet pea. Dee-licious Healthy Haddock Entrails."

She took one sniff and looked at me indignantly.

You've got to be kidding. Surely, you don't expect moi *to eat this stuff?*

"You know what the vet said last week when we went to visit, and everybody in the waiting room thought you were pregnant. Remember? She said you've really got to lose weight."

I still say she was talking to you, not me.

She jumped up on the counter and started pawing the cupboard where I keep the Bumblebee tuna.

"Forget it, Pro. You're not getting any fancy white albacore."

I scooped her down off the counter and put her back at her bowl.

"You want to be thin, don't you?"

Not if I have to eat this glop, I don't.

The vet had warned me it wasn't going to be easy. I'd just have to hang tough. Sooner or later she'd break down.

I headed for the bedroom to get dressed for my dinner date with Kandi. Prozac followed my every footstep, dodging between my ankles, all the while moaning piteously. I did my best to ignore her as I threw on some jeans, a silk shirt and an Ann Taylor blazer. But it wasn't easy, because by now, Prozac was howling like a banshee.

"Jaine? What's going on in there?"

It was my neighbor Lance, shouting from his apartment. Due to our paper-thin walls and his Superman-quality hearing, Lance knows a lot of what goes on in my life. Of course, he could've been Helen Keller and still heard Prozac's ruckus.

"Oh, it's just Prozac. She's mad at me because I put her on a diet."

"Well, keep it down, will you? Some of us are trying to have sex in here."

"I'm so sorry, Lance. I had no idea you had anyone with you."

"Who said I had anyone with me?"

Oopsie. A little more information than I needed to know.

"Have fun," I said weakly.

Then I carried Prozac out to the living room and plopped her on the sofa, where she stared up at me with Starving Orphan eyes.

"Try to understand, Pro. I'm doing this for your own good."

I bent down to kiss her, but she pulled away.

"I'm going out now to have dinner with Kandi," I said, grabbing my car keys. "I'll be back by nine. Eat your haddock."

Okay, go ahead and leave me. Go eat some fancy dinner while I'm stuck here with that disgusting haddock goop. You, of all people, have got a lot of nerve putting me on a diet! You, who just last night polished off a pint of fudge ripple ice cream. And don't think I don't know about that Chunky Monkey cone at Ben & Jerry's today.

Okay, what she actually said was *Meow,* but I could tell that's what she was thinking.

I hurried out the door before she could bring up the slice of mushroom and anchovy pizza I'd eaten for breakfast.

(Okay, two slices.)

"So what do you think? Roses or violets for the bridal bouquet?"

I was sitting across from Kandi at Pacos Tacos, our favorite Mexican restaurant, scarfing down boatloads of chips and guacamole while Kandi barely nibbled at the edge of a pickled carrot.

In the old days, she'd be telling me about some harebrained scheme to meet men. Back then, I hated those schemes. I cringed when I heard them. But now, looking back, I yearned for one of her crazy ideas, for the good old days when we were two single gals in Lalaland.

"Armando thinks I should go with violets, but I'm not sure."

"Armando? Who's Armando?"

"Didn't I tell you?" Kandi said, abandoning her carrot slice. "I hired a wedding planner. I've been so busy with *Beanie,* I haven't had much time to devote to details."

Kandi, for those of you fortunate enough never to have seen her show, is a writer for *Beanie & the Cockroach,* a stirring cartoon saga of a short-order cook named Beanie and his pet cockroach, Fred.

"If Armando thinks you should go with violets, why not take his advice? That's what you're paying him for."

"I guess you're right," Kandi said, plucking a grain of salt from a chip. "Although lately, I've been thinking freesia would be nice."

Poor Armando. Something told me he'd be earning every penny of his fee.

"Armando is just so incredibly creative; he's got the most

fabulous ideas. He thinks we should get married on the beach at sunset with champagne and gypsy violinists."

"The beach at sunset, huh?"

I could feel my hair frizzing already. Something Kandi, with her head of enviably straight chestnut hair, would never have to worry about.

"Although I was thinking," Kandi said, taking a meditative sip of her margarita, "maybe it should be margaritas and a mariachi band."

And so it went, through dinner—Kandi floating along on a cloud of wedding plans, yammering endlessly about the invitations, the flowers, the musicians, the bridal gown. And, of course, the most important part of the wedding, the fiancé. I heard what an angel Steve was, how sweet, how kind, how caring. I heard how, unlike some men, he didn't go screaming into the night at the thought of planning a wedding with his bride-to-be. Apparently, he was a good sport about the whole thing. In fact, that's where he was tonight, with Armando, choosing his tuxedo.

"Really, Jaine, he doesn't mind a bit when I talk about the wedding."

I was glad he didn't mind. It was all I could to do keep from dozing off into my refried beans.

"Oh, by the way," Kandi said, "I almost forgot the reason why I wanted to see you. I ordered the most fabulous bridesmaid gowns!"

She reached into her purse and took out a picture she'd ripped from a magazine.

"Here," she said, handing me the picture. "Armando and I decided to go with the traditional look. Isn't it divine?"

Omigod. I took a desperate gulp of my margarita. It was a bridesmaid's nightmare. Big puffy sleeves. Tiny pinched-in waist. And a billowing hip-enlarging skirt. All of it in a nauseating baby pink.

Kandi smiled eagerly. "It's the Cinderella look."

Just what I always wanted to look like: Cinderella on steroids.

"So? What do you think? Isn't it terrific?"

Horrific would be more like it, but I managed a sickly smile and nodded yes. But as it happened, Kandi didn't notice my sickly smile because at that moment, Steve showed up at our table. I could see once more why Kandi had fallen for him. He was, in no uncertain terms, a cutie. Spiky Hugh Grant hair, chocolate-brown eyes, a heartmeltingly sweet smile, and buns to die for.

Kandi's eyes lit up with love.

"Hi, honey," she said, as he bent down to kiss her. "What are you doing here?"

"Armando and I finished early, so I thought I'd join you two."

"That's great. Isn't that great, Jaine?"

For the second time in less than two minutes, I pasted a sickly smile on my face. "Yeah, great."

Steve grabbed a chair, and the next thing I knew, he and Kandi were holding hands over their dessert flans and undoubtedly playing footsie under the table. Once again, I was demoted to fifth wheel.

Kandi gazed at Steve, gooey-eyed.

"Jaine just loves her bridesmaid dress. Don't you, Jaine?"

"Just love it."

And then I did the only thing I could do under the circumstances: Finish every last morsel of my flan. (And theirs, too, if you must know.)

I sneaked into my apartment like a cheating lover and raced to the bathroom to brush my teeth before Prozac could smell the chimichangas on my breath. I was hoping to convince her I'd had a low-cal tuna nicoise for dinner.

But Prozac wasn't having anything to do with me. She stared at me through slitted eyes and wriggled out of my arms when

I tried to pick her up. I checked her dinner bowl. She hadn't touched a bite.

"Prozac, sweetie, you've got to eat something."

I'll eat when you feed me something that doesn't look like recycled upchuck.

I had to admit, it did look pretty disgusting.

"Here. I'll sprinkle some kitty treats on top."

I grabbed a can of cat treats and tossed a liberal handful on top of the diet food. Anything to get her to give the stuff a try.

Prozac sniffed at the bowl dismissively.

I'd rather have bacon bits was what I think she was trying to say.

Bacon bits are Prozac's favorite snack, right along with pizza anchovies and Chicken McNuggets.

"You can't have bacon bits," I said. "They're not good for you. C'mon now. You love your kitty treats."

Not that night, she didn't. She eyed them disdainfully, then stalked off to the living room.

Call me when you've got something worth eating.

"Okay, be that way," I shouted after her. "I'm not going to weaken. For your information, there are starving kitties in Asia who'd love to have Healthy Haddock Entrails for dinner!"

Usually Prozac snuggles up next to me when I watch TV in bed at night, belching fish fumes in my face. But that night she stayed alone and aloof on the living room sofa.

I figured eventually she'd wander in, but three hours later, there was still no sign of her. I turned out the light, but sleep wouldn't come. I tried watching some mind-numbing infomercials, but they failed to make me even remotely drowsy. It looked like I was in for a sleepless night. I missed Prozac's warm, furry body nuzzled under my neck. I tried cuddling with a pillow, but all I got were feathers up my nose. This would never do.

"Prozac, honey," I called out. "Come to bed."

Nothing.

I went out to where she was sleeping, like a displaced husband, on the living room sofa. I scooped her in my arms, but she wasn't having any of it. In an instant, she was back down on the floor, glaring up at me.

"Prozac, come back to bed. *Please*. Mommy needs her sleep."

You should have thought of that when you fed me that Haddock glop.

Then she jumped back up on the sofa and curled into an angry ball.

And so, with a weary sigh, I shuffled off to the kitchen, where I proceeded to fix her a bowl of fancy white albacore. With bacon bits on top.

She could always start her diet tomorrow.

YOU'VE GOT MAIL

To: Jausten
From: Shoptillyoudrop
Subject: America's Most Irritating

Jaine, honey—

Sit down for this one. You won't believe what your father is up to now.

The absolutely nicest man has moved to Tampa Vistas, Jim Sternmuller, a retired minister from Minnesota. Just the sweetest, kindest man you could ever hope to meet, and a widower, to boot. All the single ladies have been tripping over themselves bringing casseroles to his townhouse.

But for some insane reason, your father is convinced that he's seen Reverend Sternmuller on *America's Most Wanted!* He says he's the Hugo Boss Strangler, a madman who runs around strangling women with Hugo Boss ties. Have you ever heard of anything so ridiculous? For one thing, Reverend Sternmuller doesn't even wear ties. Usually he wears tasteful jersey-knit sports shirts, the kind I'd love your father to wear, but Daddy says his raggedy old T-shirts are good enough for him.

And now Daddy is determined to "unmask" Reverend Sternmuller and bring him to justice!

Where your father gets these crazy ideas I'll never know. There's no way on earth that Reverend Sternmuller is one of America's Most Wanted. Although your father is far and away America's Most Irritating.

Your frazzled,
Mom

To: Jausten
From: DaddyO
Subject: The Nose Knows

Hi, Lambchop—

Has Mom told you the big news? We've got a mass murderer in Tampa Vistas, some guy passing himself off as a retired minister. But I recognized him the minute I saw him. He's the Hugo Boss Strangler. Kills all his victims with a designer tie.

Your mom thinks I'm crazy, but I know what I saw, and I saw "Reverend Sternmuller" on *America's Most Wanted*. Besides, I've got a nose for these things. I can smell a bad guy a mile off.

Your mom thinks that just because he doesn't wear Hugo Boss ties, he's not the Hugo Boss Strangler. Well, of course he wouldn't wear the ties in public. He's probably got them hidden somewhere in his townhouse.

Trust me, sweet pea. The Nose knows!

Your loving,
Daddy

To: Jausten
From: Shoptillyoudrop
Subject: P.S.

P.S. I've been so upset with Daddy, I ordered a 360-day supply of Stress-Less vitamin pills from the Shopping Channel, only $36.99 plus shipping and handling. And while I was at it, I picked up the most adorable Calvin Kleinman capri pants set. With little martinis all over it. It's perfect for L.A. Should I order one for you, too?

Love and kisses,
Mom

To: Shoptillyoudrop
From: Jausten

Thanks, Mom, but I think I'll pass on the Calvin Kleinman. When it comes to martinis, I prefer mine in a glass.

And try not to worry about Daddy. This Reverend Sternmuller thing is probably just another Whim du Jour. I bet he's already forgotten all about it.

To: Jausten
From: DaddyO

I just called *America's Most Wanted* and tipped them off to the Reverend, but who knows how long it will take for them to do anything?

In the meanwhile, he could strike again right here in Tampa Vistas. So I guess it's up to your old Daddy to stop him!

Wish me luck, honey. "The Nose" won't rest until he's brought the Hugo Boss Strangler to justice!

To: Shoptillyoudrop
From: Jausten
Subject: Stress-Less Pills

Dear Mom,

On second thought, better have those Stress-Less pills shipped overnight.

Chapter 3

I drove over to Pam Kenton's apartment the next night, my mind still reeling from my parents' e-mails.

Can you believe Daddy, and his insane conviction that his new neighbor was one of "America's Most Wanted"? I shouldn't have been surprised. Daddy's imagination has always been in overdrive. This is a man who insists he once saw Mother Teresa buying thong underwear at Victoria's Secret.

There'd be trouble ahead, no doubt about it. My father attracts trouble like white cashmere attracts wine stains. I just thanked my lucky stars I was 3,000 miles out of his orbit.

I pulled up in front of the address Pam had given me, a great old Spanish-style apartment building in the heart of Hollywood. Built sometime in the 1920s, it had balconies and balustrades and an authentic Spanish red-tile roof.

Unfortunately, the inside of the building was a lot less impressive than the outside. Whoever owned it clearly was not spending anything on upkeep.

I headed up the chipped tile stairs to Pam's apartment. The stairwell reeked of cabbage. I sure hoped it wasn't part of the dinner Pam had promised me in exchange for helping her with her resume.

I rang the bell and Pam answered the door in sweats and

Reeboks, clearly a graduate of the Jaine Austen School of Dressing.

"Hi, there," she beamed. "It's so sweet of you to help me with my resume like this."

"Think nothing of it," I said, still kicking myself for not charging her.

"I told everyone in the PMS Club that I'm bringing you to the meeting tonight. They can't wait to meet you. Now c'mon in and I'll give you the grand tour."

She ushered me into a huge room with a high vaulted ceiling and French doors leading out onto a balcony.

"This is the living room," she said. "And the bedroom. And the study. And the den. And the library."

"Oh, it's a studio apartment."

"Yep. Come see the bedroom."

She led me to the corner of the room, and there, behind a Victorian screen, was an old brass bed with what looked like a hand-sewn quilt and a platoon of kitschy souvenir throw pillows. I loved the way she mixed Victoriana with Americana and topped it off with junk shop finds. The whole place was like that, an eclectic mix of furniture, most of which I suspected she'd picked up at second-hand stores.

I admire people who can throw different styles together and have it come out looking good. When they do it, it's eclectic. When I do it, it's a mess.

"Your place is fantastic," I said, taking it all in.

"But wait," she said. "The tour's not over yet. You haven't seen the Pam Kenton Hall of Fame."

I followed her across the room.

"Voila!" she said, opening the door to her vintage bathroom, with its badly cracked original tile and fixtures that were installed back when Fatty Arbuckle was in diapers.

"It's sure got a lot of character," I said.

"I'd prefer some water pressure, but I guess I'll have to settle for character."

"So where's the hall of fame?"

"Here," she said, pointing to a wall covered with 8x10 framed glossies. "Here I am, in all my theatrical triumphs."

I stepped closer to get a better look.

"Here's me as Stella in *A Streetcar Named Desire*."

"Wow, that's great. Was that on Broadway?"

"No, off Broadway. About 3,000 miles off Broadway, at the West Covina Community Playhouse. Oh, here's me as Hedda Gabler. And here's me as Felix Unger in my high school production of *The Odd Couple*."

"You played Felix Unger?"

"It was an all-girls school. I look good in a mustache, don't you think? It's nice to know, for when menopause sets in. Oh, and here's my all-time favorite—me as an eggplant in a vegetable soup commercial."

"Very impressive."

"Sad to say, but that was the high point of my career. The spot went national, and I made some really nice money from it.

"Oh, well," she sighed, leading me back to her studio. "Enough of my showbiz years. Time to get back to reality and work on my resume. Can I get you some wine?"

I shook my head.

"I really shouldn't. Not if I want to keep a clear head."

"You're absolutely right. So what do you want? Red or white?"

"Red."

"Great."

She scooted over to her "bar," a wrought-iron bistro table sporting a dusty jug of Costco gin and a couple of bottles of screw-top wine.

"Want to smell the cork?" she asked, tossing me the screw top.

I laughed as she poured us both some wine.

We settled down on her large chintz sofa and got to work on her resume.

"So what sort of work experience have you had?" I asked, taking notes on a steno pad.

"Well, there's the waitressing. But I can't use that."

"Sure you can."

She looked dubious. "Waitress doesn't sound very impressive."

"No, but Food Service Specialist does."

She nodded happily. "So it does."

"What else?" I asked.

"I've done some temp filing."

"Organizational Engineer," I jotted down. "What else?"

"When I was a kid, I sold Girl Scout cookies."

"Professional Fund-raiser."

By now she was beaming. "Hey, you're really good at this stuff."

Pam filled me in on the details of her job history, and I told her I'd finish the resume by the end of the week.

"Are you sure I can't pay you?"

Yes! Tell her yes! You want some money!

But like a fool, I said, "Forget it. It's nothing. I knock these things out in my sleep."

"You're a doll," she said, with a grateful smile. "Now let me get our dinner."

She got up and went behind some beaded curtains into her tiny box of a kitchen.

"There's always plenty to eat at the club," she called out from behind the curtain, "so I just fixed us a light bite."

She came out from the kitchen holding two sacks from Burger King.

"Which means only one order of fries with our Whoppers."

Then, grinning, she set out burgers, fries, and Cokes on the ottoman she used as a coffee table.

"Hope you don't mind my doing takeout. I'm not much of a cook."

"Me, neither," I said. "I use my oven to warm my socks."

"Really? I use mine to dry my newspapers."

Clearly Emeril had nothing to fear from us.

"Besides," I said, squeezing ketchup onto my burger, "I adore Whoppers."

And that was no lie. I proceeded to dig into mine with gusto. And I was not alone in my gustohood. Pam was right alongside me, mouthful for mouthful.

When we finally came up for air, we started gabbing. I told Pam about my life as a writer, and she told me about her life as an actress. And trust me, I had the better deal. I don't know how actors cope with all the rejection. Would you believe she was once turned down for the part of a corpse because she didn't look dead enough?

Pam asked me about my love life and, after a hearty chuckle, I explained that it was currently on the endangered species list. I told her about my disastrous marriage to The Blob. That's what I call my ex-husband. He seemed perfectly divine when I met him. Not a flaw in sight. No hint of the man who would eventually pick his teeth with paper clips and watch ESPN during sex.

She tsk-tsked in sympathy.

"I know just how you feel. My marriage was a fiasco, too."

"Really? What went wrong?"

"Everything. We fought constantly, bickered, had screaming matches, threw lamps at each other. And that was just on the honeymoon."

She popped a final fry into her mouth, then checked her watch.

"We'd better get going, or we'll be late for the meeting. Time to do the dishes!"

She held out a wastepaper basket, and we tossed in our trash.

"Well, that's done," she said, wiping her hands on her sweats, clearly a graduate of the Jaine Austen School of Housekeeping, too.

Pam drove her battered Nissan Sentra west on Sunset to Brentwood.

"So tell me more about the club," I said, as we tooled past the quatrillion-dollar estates on Sunset Boulevard.

"Well, we've been meeting for about a year now. Most of us hooked up at the L.A. Racquet Club."

"The fancy gym on the west side?"

Pam nodded. "I'd just finished shooting my vegetable soup commercial and I was feeling flush. So I sprung for a membership."

"Isn't it awfully snooty?"

"Some of the members are, but the PMS gals are really great. We connected right away."

"Tell me about them."

"Let's see. There's Rochelle. She hosts the meetings every week."

"Every week? Doesn't she mind?"

"Hell, no. She insists on it. She loves to play hostess. I think she's memorized every book Martha Stewart ever wrote. The woman cooks everything from scratch. If she could make her own water, she would. She puts cocktail umbrellas in her margaritas and little Mexican flags in her homemade empanadas."

"Little Mexican flags?"

"I know. It's unbelievable. But I've got to say she makes the best damn guacamole I ever tasted. She says her secret ingredient is a dash of orange juice. Whatever it is, it's fantastic."

"So is this Rochelle the ringleader of the group?"

"Oh, no. Far from it. That's the funny thing about Rochelle. As much as she loves to entertain, she's really quite shy. Just flits around, taking margarita orders, making sure everybody has enough to eat. She tends to blend in with the wallpaper, but she's very sweet. Always sympathetic when one of us has a problem. In her own quiet way, she's the glue that holds the group together."

"What about the other club members?"

"Like I said, they're all terrific." Then she frowned. "Except maybe Marybeth."

"Who's Marybeth?"

"Interior decorator. Very successful."

"What's wrong with her?"

"You'll find out soon enough," she said, turning onto a leafy street. "We're here."

She parked in front of an impressive colonial house, gleaming toothpaste white in the moonlight.

I whistled softly. "Nice house."

"It's Rochelle's pride and joy. She's constantly redecorating. I don't think there's an original room left. My theory is that the house is a substitute for kids."

"Oh?"

"She and her husband haven't been able to conceive, and she pours all her maternal energy into the house."

"Very interesting."

"Just call me Dr. Freud. Too bad I can't fix my own neuroses." She snapped off the ignition and turned to me with a grin. "Guess it's time to hit those margaritas."

And so I sucked in my gut, poufed out my hair, and headed off to my first meeting of the PMS Club.

Chapter 4

Rochelle Meyers may have been obsessed with her house, but she sure didn't take any pains with herself. She greeted us at the door in baggy jeans and an oversized denim work shirt, a dishtowel slung over her shoulder. Her wispy brown hair was in desperate need of a good styling and I couldn't help noticing a bit of a tummy underneath that work shirt.

"Hi." She smiled shyly, her face flushed. "You must be Jaine. I'm Rochelle. Come on in."

She ushered us into a foyer the size of my dining room.

"Why don't you girls get settled in the living room? I've still got a few things to take care of in the kitchen."

And with that, she scurried off down the hall.

"She's always got something to take care of in the kitchen," Pam said, leading me into a huge beige-and-white living room, tastefully decorated, with a massive stone fireplace and twin sofas the size of railway cars.

A slim, gray-haired woman in her sixties was sitting on one of the sofas, reaching for a cut-glass bowl filled to the brim with plump macadamia nuts. I eyed the nuts hungrily. I couldn't wait to grab some.

(Yes, I know I'd just finished a Whopper with fries. What can I say? I'm disgraceful.)

"Hi, Doris," Pam said to the gray-haired woman. "Meet my friend Jaine. Jaine, this is Doris Jenkins."

"Welcome to the madhouse," Doris grinned.

Like Pam and Rochelle, she wore hardly any make-up, making no attempt to cover the laugh lines that gave her face a comfortable lived-in look.

I plopped down on the sofa and helped myself to a handful of macadamias.

"Jaine's a writer," Pam said. "She's helping me with my resume."

"A writer? Really? I'm impressed. Writing's like pulling teeth for me."

"Me, too," I said. "But that doesn't stop me.

"So," I said, popping a nut in my mouth, "Pam tells me you guys all met at the L.A. Racquet Club."

"That's right," Doris said. "I remember it well. I'd just dropped 185 pounds of ugly flab."

"Really?"

"Yeah. I got divorced."

It was an old gag, but it cracked her up. She laughed, a loud, raucous laugh.

"Happiest day of my life, getting rid of that bum."

At which point, an exceedingly attractive guy in his twenties came sailing into the room with a tray of margaritas. I blinked in surprise. What was a guy doing here?

"You must be Jaine Austen," he said, setting the margaritas on the coffee table. "Love your books."

Usually I groan when people hand me that line, but this time I found myself smiling. There was something about this guy that I liked. Not in a sexual way, though. My lightning powers of deduction told me he was gay.

Especially when he said, "I'm Colin Lambert, the club's token gay guy."

"How did you meet the others in the club?" I asked. "Do you belong to the racquet club, too?"

"Oh, no. I'm Marybeth's indentured servant. Well, technically I'm her design assistant. But it feels more like slave labor when she calls me at three in the morning and asks me to 'skedaddle' over to her place with some fabric swatches. Which is what she did last night. No joke. Three in the morning."

He sank into the sofa with a sigh.

"I need a drink," he said, reaching for a margarita.

"So do I, sweetie!" boomed a loud whiskey voice. "So do I!"

I looked up and saw a tall blonde with big hair, big lips, and big boobs to match. She looked like she was in her early thirties, but this was L.A., the plastic surgery capital of the world. For all I knew, she was on Medicare. She swept across the room in a cloud of expensive perfume.

"Sorry I'm late. Shoe sale at Ferragamo. So many slingbacks, so little time."

She grabbed a margarita, tossed the paper umbrella aside, and practically inhaled it in one gulp.

"Jaine," Pam said, "this is Ashley, our resident shopaholic."

"Pleased to meet you, hon." She kicked off her shoes and grinned. "Pam says you're our kind of people."

I smiled what I hoped was an our-kind-of-people smile.

"Where's Rochelle?" she asked, looking around the room.

"In the kitchen," Pam said. "As usual."

"Rochelle!" Ashley shouted. "Get your fanny out here! You can't stay in the kitchen all night!"

"I'm coming," Rochelle called from the kitchen.

Seconds later, she came bustling out with a bowl of the most delicious-looking guacamole I'd ever seen, studded with giant chunks of avocado. Between the macadamia nuts and the avocado, I'd just died and gone to calorie heaven.

"I hope it's not too spicy," Rochelle said, her brow furrowed with concern.

"It's never too spicy, Rochelle," Colin said. "It's always wonderful."

She set the bowl down on the coffee table and we all attacked it, swooping down with our chips like vultures.

"It's divine," I said. And it was.

"You sure it's not too spicy?"

"No, it's not spicy at all."

"Is it spicy enough?"

"Rochelle, it's great!" Pam said. "Now sit down and have a margarita and stop obsessing."

"Wait. I've got to get the empanadas."

Before I knew it, she was trotting out from the kitchen with a platter of homemade empanadas, cooked to flaky perfection. Each one sporting a miniature Mexican flag.

"I hope they're not soggy," Rochelle said, with a frown.

"Rochelle!" Pam forced her down onto the sofa and handed her a margarita.

"Drink," she commanded.

Rochelle took a sip.

"Now relax and get tootled like the rest of us."

"Somebody pass the empanadas!" Doris said. "Let's dig in."

"Aren't we going to wait for Marybeth?" Rochelle asked.

"Don't be silly," Colin said. "That could take forever. You know how she likes to make a grand entrance." He turned to me to explain. "Marybeth always waits till she's sure everybody's here and then comes bursting in with some 'yummy news.'"

"Is that how she describes it? Yummy news?"

"Unfortunately, yes." Pam rolled her eyes. "Marybeth is the most relentlessly perky person I've ever met."

"Yeah," Colin said. "Like Shirley Temple on uppers."

"It's true," Ashley said, reaching for another margarita. "I think she's mainlining antidepressants."

"She's always giving us lectures about how we're supposed to look on the bright side," Pam said. "If she tells me to look on the bright side one more time, I'm gonna shove my Mexican flag up her wazoo."

"You guys are horrible," said Rochelle. "Don't listen to them, Jaine. Marybeth is a wonderful person. She's been helping me redecorate my master bath for the past six months, and she's been so much fun to work with."

Everyone groaned.

"Okay, so maybe she's a little too upbeat sometimes, but basically Marybeth is a warm, caring person."

"She's caring, all right," Colin said. "That's why she called me on my cell phone in the middle of my cousin's wedding to tell me to bring her a frappucino."

"Shh," Doris whispered. "I think I hear her coming up the path."

Sure enough, the doorbell rang.

"She always rings the bell," Pam said, "even though she knows the door's open. She has to announce her arrival."

"Come on in," Rochelle called out.

A subtle tension filled the air. And then Marybeth Olson blew into the room.

She wasn't at all what I'd expected. I'd seen my share of decorators on House & Garden Television, all of them sleek and sophisticated and bone thin. But Marybeth looked like she'd just stepped off a dairy farm. Fresh scrubbed and clean-cut, with squeaky-clean blonde hair and the most startling green eyes I'd ever seen, as green as a pair of my mom's fake emerald earrings. The only make-up on her face was some candy red lipstick. And although she wasn't the least bit fat, she was far from the social string bean I thought she'd be.

When Pam introduced us, she took my hand and greeted me warmly.

"I'm sooo happy you could join us, Judy."

"Actually, it's Jaine."

"Sorry," she said, flashing me a dazzling smile. "I always get my *J* names mixed up."

Then she wedged herself onto the sofa between Doris and Colin, subtly forcing Colin to move down to the end of the sofa.

"Have a margarita, Marybeth," Rochelle said. "And some guacamole." She popped up and passed the guacamole to Marybeth.

Marybeth laid another kilowatt smile on Rochelle. "It looks delicious."

"I hope it's not too spicy."

"*It's not too spicy!*" everyone shouted.

"Okay, ladies and gentleman," Doris said, clinking her cocktail umbrella against her margarita glass. "The weekly meeting of the honorable PMS Club is now called to order. Any news?"

Without missing a beat, Marybeth piped up, "I've got yummy news!"

Pam poked me in the ribs.

"The other day, just for a lark, I decided to buy a lottery ticket, and you'll never guess what happened!"

"You won?" Pam blinked, incredulous.

"Yes!" Marybeth rummaged around her purse and fished out a lottery ticket. "Isn't it wonderful?" She kissed the ticket with her candy red lips. "It's not very much, though. Just fifty thou."

Just fifty thou?

"The rich get richer," Pam muttered under her breath.

That might not have been much to Marybeth, but it was a lot of Whoppers for a gal like me.

"That's great!" Rochelle said, beaming.

The others murmured congratulations with a marked lack of enthusiasm.

"Anybody else have any yummy news?" Doris asked.

"Actually, I do have good news," Pam said. "Jaine here has agreed to write a resume for me."

"Here's to Jaine!" Ashley took a healthy slug of her margarita. Something told me she would have toasted Hitler if she thought she could get another drink out of it.

"That's the good news," Pam continued. "The bad news is that I got rejected for another part this week. The casting director kept me waiting three hours and then didn't even bother to have me read. She said they'd already decided to go with someone else. It wouldn't have been so bad, only they'd made the decision two hours earlier and nobody told me. She made me sit there all afternoon for nothing. And she didn't even apologize."

The members of the PMS Club were filled with righteous indignation.

"What a horrible person!" Colin said. Well, that's not exactly what he said. He said a four-letter word that rhymes with *blunt*. (Those of you who guessed *runt*, guess again.)

"Here's to that [bleepity bleep] casting director." Ashley raised her glass in another toast. "May she get a yeast infection!"

We all raised our glasses and drank to that most heartfelt toast.

"So what else is new?" Ashley asked.

"Well," Doris said, taking a deep breath, "I went out on a date this weekend. From a video dating service."

"Tell all," Colin said.

"What a nightmare. The guy wrote on his member profile that he was 62. And I'm sure he was 62—twenty years ago. All I know is he was at least 80 when I saw him on Saturday. What a date. I spent the whole night slapping him."

I blinked, incredulous. "To keep him off you?"

"No, to wake him up."

"You think that's bad?" Colin says. "Remember that guy I gave my phone number to at Williams Sonoma? The one who looked like Kyan on *Queer Eye*? Well, he called."

"But that's great," Rochelle said.

"Not so great. He turned out to be an insurance salesman.

I bought $25,000 worth of term life before I found out he was married with three kids."

"Here's to the life insurance salesman," said Ashley. "May he catch the casting lady's yeast infection."

And we all drank to that one, too.

Pam was right about the club. I was enjoying myself immensely. I only hoped that I could get through the evening without having to talk about myself. As nice a bunch as they appeared to be, I wasn't totally comfortable spilling my guts to them. Not yet, anyway. But it looked like I was going to be in the spotlight, after all. Because just then I saw Marybeth gazing at me appraisingly.

"What about you, Julie? What's going on in your life?"

"Actually, it's Jaine."

"Oh, gosh. Forgive me. I am so bad with names. I'm surprised I still have any clients left."

"Me, too," I heard Colin mutter under his breath.

Marybeth shot me a smile that was meant to be sympathetic. "Go on. Tell us what's happening in your life. Any men?"

Why did I get the feeling that she already knew the truth about me, that I was just another manless gal in L.A., whose last date was a distant memory, and an unpleasant one at that?

"Actually, I've been dating an actor. He's sort of famous. I really shouldn't tell tales out of school, but what the hell? His initials are Denzel Washington."

Okay, so I didn't say that. I just smiled and made a passing reference to the fact that the landscape of my social life resembled a nuclear wasteland, and the others turned their attention to Rochelle.

"So, Rochelle," Doris asked, "how are things with Marty?"

Rochelle jumped up and started for the kitchen.

"Who wants more empanadas?"

"Rochelle," Doris barked. "Get back here."

Rochelle sat back down on the sofa with a sigh. Marybeth reached over and took her hand.

"C'mon, honey," she said. "You can tell us. That's what we're here for."

Rochelle shot her a grateful look, then took a deep breath.

"Things with Marty aren't so hot. He hardly talks to me. He comes home at all hours. Says he's working late. I just don't understand it. What sort of dentist works till midnight?"

She shook her head unhappily and stared down at her nails, which I could see were bitten to the quick.

"When he comes home, the first thing he does is head for the shower. I heard on *Oprah* the other day that's a sign that your husband is having an affair."

She looked up from her nails.

"What do you think?" she asked, her eyes wide with worry. "Do you think Marty's having an affair?"

Nobody said anything. Nobody had the heart to say what they were thinking, that of course he was having an affair, that she should wake up and smell the cappuccino and get the name of a good divorce attorney.

"It's hard to tell, Rochelle," Pam finally managed to say.

"Men." Ashley stared morosely into her margarita. "What a bunch of bums. At least after I caught my husband cheating on me with our 17-year-old neighbor, he had the good grace to die and leave me a boatload of money."

She raised her glass in a toast.

"Here's to my husband Roger. If there are yeast infections in hell, I hope he gets one."

"Here, here!" said Pam, and we all raised our glasses.

Marybeth tsk-tsked in disapproval.

"You guys are terrible. Such Negative Nellies. For your information, there are plenty of good men out there. In fact, it just so happens I've found not one, but *two* of them."

"I suppose you're going to tell us all about them," Pam sighed wearily.

Marybeth reached for the bowl of macadamias, which I'd pretty much demolished. "Pass the nuts will you, June?"

"I'm afraid I ate most of them," I said, passing her the bowl.

"That's all right," Rochelle said, jumping up. "I've got more in the kitchen."

"Don't bother, honey," Marybeth said. "There're still a few left." Emphasis on *a few.*

By now, I was firmly entrenched in the anti-Marybeth camp.

Marybeth rifled through the nuts carefully. "There aren't any peanuts in here, are there, Rochelle?"

"Heavens, no, Marybeth. No peanuts. Just macadamias. You know I'd never serve you peanuts."

I shot Pam a puzzled look.

"Marybeth's allergic to peanuts," she explained.

Satisfied that there were no offending peanuts in the bowl, Marybeth popped a macadamia in her mouth and made us wait while she chewed and swallowed before telling us about her two good men.

The first was a decorator she'd met on a recent trip to New York.

"Rene is an absolute genius," she gushed. "And you'll never guess what he's going to do!"

"You're right, Marybeth," Pam said. "We'll never guess. So why don't you tell us?"

"He's going to move to L.A. and be my partner! Isn't that the most marvelous news?"

Everyone agreed, with a distinct lack of enthusiasm, that it was marvelous news. Everyone except Colin, who didn't even bother to paste a phony smile on his face. On the contrary, his jaw was clenched tight with anger.

"And now for the best news of all!" Marybeth beamed. What a build-up. I was surprised she hadn't arranged for a fanfare of trumpets.

"I've met a man!"

"That's wonderful," Rochelle said, a genuine smile on her face, the only genuine smile in the room. "When did this happen?"

"Oh, I've been seeing him for a few months now."

"And you haven't said anything to us?"

"I didn't want to jinx it. I wanted to make sure it was the real thing." Marybeth beamed. "And it is. We're going to be married!"

Everyone murmured their congratulations, except for Colin, who was still stone-faced with anger. If Marybeth noticed, she didn't say anything.

"We're so in love," she gushed. "So madly in love."

"Tell us all about him," Rochelle said.

But Marybeth just smiled coyly.

"No, not yet. I'll save that for next week."

Ashley sighed, exasperated. "It's just like you, Marybeth, to keep us waiting all week."

"Oh, don't be such an old gwouch," Marybeth said, pursing her candy red lips into a perfect pout.

Ugh. Colin was right. She really was Shirley Temple on uppers.

Pardon me while I fwow up.

Soon after Marybeth's announcement, the last of the margaritas was slurped and the meeting broke up. Pam started clearing dishes from the coffee table, and the rest of us joined in.

"Really, girls," Rochelle said. "I can clean up myself."

"We know you can," Pam said, "but you're not going to."

I helped the others in the kitchen and then excused myself to go to the bathroom.

I was heading down the corridor toward the bathroom when I saw Colin in the dining room, talking on his cell phone. Snoop that I am, I stopped to listen.

"I'd like to kill that bitch," I heard him hiss. "She promised she'd make me her partner."

So. That explained why he'd been so angry.

It's funny, I thought, as I sniffed the triple-milled French soap in Rochelle's guest bathroom, except for Rochelle, there wasn't a single person in the PMS Club who was happy for Marybeth.

For someone who preached positive thinking, she sure managed to stir up a lot of negative energy.

After thanking Rochelle and assuring her once more that her guacamole wasn't too spicy, we headed for our cars. It was quite an impressive assortment. Doris drove an Audi; Colin, a BMW; Ashley, a Jag; and Marybeth, a Porsche. (True, Colin's BMW was at least ten years old, but it *was* a BMW.) Clearly Pam and I were the low-rent members of this group.

Colin bid us all a curt good-bye and got into his car.

"Nighty-nite, Colin," Marybeth waved.

"Nighty-frigging-nite," Colin muttered. Only he didn't use the word *frigging*.

"What's wrong with him?" Marybeth said, all wide-eyed innocence, as he drove off. "Oh, well. Whatever it is, he'll get over it. He always does."

Then she hopped into her silver Porsche, waved good-bye to us with two limp fingers, and sped away.

I watched in amazement as she roared down the street, tires squealing, rubber burning. I'd seen more conservative driving at Indianapolis. She sure as heck wasn't getting any Good Driver Discounts.

"The woman is an accident waiting to happen," Pam said, shaking her head. "I'm surprised she hasn't wound up in a ditch somewhere."

"You know what I can't believe?" Doris said. "I can't believe she brought in that guy from New York to be her partner. After all these years of promising Colin she'd give him the job."

"That's Marybeth for you," Ashley shrugged.

Doris sighed in agreement, and the two of them got into their cars.

After they'd driven off, Pam turned to me and beamed.

"Guess what? We all talked it over while you were in the bathroom, and we want you to join the club!"

"Really?"

"So how about it?"

I have to admit, I was flattered. The last thing I'd been asked to join was Macy's Pantyhose Club. (Buy ten pair, and you get the eleventh free.) And now that Kandi was abandoning me for the altar, I was definitely in the market for some new friends. Not to mention some free margaritas. So what if Marybeth was a pill? The others were a lot of fun.

And so, in a move I'd live to deeply regret, I said yes.

Chapter 5

O f course, at the time, I didn't have an inkling of all the PMS crappola that would eventually be hitting my fan.

My biggest concern then was my interview at Union National Bank. It had been ages since I worked with a major corporate client. My last job interview had been with a far less impressive outfit—Big Al's Moving & Storage Company, for a plum assignment writing Big Al's Yellow Pages ad.

As I rode up in the elevator of the Union National building the next day, butterflies frolicked gaily in my stomach. I stepped onto the executive floor and found myself in what looked like a British gentlemen's club: gleaming hardwood floors dotted with Persian rugs, overstuffed leather club chairs, and—in the center of it all—an aristocratic gray-haired receptionist, with a hawklike nose and cheekbones sharp enough to open envelopes.

I approached her desk, an immaculate cherry wood table with absolutely nothing on it except a phone and a vase of perfect roses. I cleared my throat and told her I was there for a ten o'clock meeting with Andrew Ferguson. She looked me up and down, giving me the royal once-over, like Queen Elizabeth inspecting one of her dogs for fleas. I was glad I was wearing my Prada pantsuit.

(Yes, I, Jaine Austen of Bargain Barn fame, actually own a Prada pantsuit, a souvenir of a murder I was involved in last year, one you can read all about in *Shoes to Die For,* now available in paperback at a bookstore near you.)

If I do say so myself, I looked rather spiffy. Thank goodness Queen Elizabeth couldn't see that underneath my Prada jacket, my Prada pants were unbuttoned at the waist.

The Queen nodded curtly and, in a British accent I suspect she'd picked up from watching old Greer Garson movies, said, "Take a seat, please. Mr. Ferguson will see you shortly."

I took a seat as instructed, reminding myself that under no circumstances was I to open my suit jacket and reveal my unbuttoned waistband.

Every time I thought about that waistband I wanted to strangle Prozac. It was all her fault that my tummy was hanging out in an unsightly roll. I'd planned on wearing a new pair of control-top pantyhose, one with a built-in "waist nipper." I'd laid them out on my bed before I hopped into the shower that morning, but when I came out, they were gone.

Prozac hid them, of course. I could tell by the self-satisfied smirk on her face as she watched me search for the missing hose. I'd decided to put her back on her diet that morning, and clearly this was her way of getting revenge.

I'd checked under the bed and behind the sofa cushions, two of her favorite hiding places. No sign of the pantyhose. She probably buried them under her kitty litter. She did that once to my bra when she was mad at me for being late with her dinner. I couldn't face the sight of my twenty-dollar pantyhose buried under cat poop, so I'd grabbed a pair of stretched-out knee highs, finished dressing, and hurried off to my meeting with Andrew Ferguson.

I checked my watch. Quarter past ten. Queen Elizabeth was staring off into space, avoiding my gaze, determined not to engage in idle chatter with the likes of me.

I should've used the time to go over my research on Union National, but I was too busy being irritated about the roll of fat pressing against my waistband that wouldn't have been there if I'd been wearing my waist-nipper pantyhose.

"Ms. Austen?"

I looked up, and all thoughts of my flab flew out the window.

Standing before me was a dollburger of the highest order. Tall and slim, with the boyish good looks I have a particular weakness for. No studly guys with megamuscles for me. I prefer the sensitive, artistic, 99-pound weakling variety of guy. I guess it must be an Opposites Attract kind of thing. Anyhow, whatever I was attracted to, this guy had it in spades.

"I'm Andrew Ferguson," he said, holding out his hand. "Pleased to meet you."

I don't know how long I stood there staring at his Adam's apple before I realized I was supposed to be shaking his hand. But finally I caught on and murmured something exceptionally clever like, "Um. Me, too."

I followed him back to his office, fascinated by the way his sandy brown hair curled at the nape of his neck.

Good heavens. I'd only felt this kind of attraction to three other men in my life. One turned out to be a lying sociopath. The other turned out to be studying for the priesthood. And the third turned out to be The Blob, a man who actually wore flip-flops to our wedding. So you can see that I haven't had a great track record when it comes to guys who make my G-spot sing. Which is why I decided right then and there to rein in any and all lustful feelings for Andrew Ferguson.

It wasn't easy, but I almost managed to ignore his crooked smile and pay attention as he told me about the job as freelance editor of the bank's monthly newsletter.

"You'd write employee profiles. You know, employee-of-the-month kind of thing. The branch managers would supply you with news items about promotions. And we'd expect you to cover any events the bank sponsors. What do you think? Sound like something you'd be interested in?"

"That depends. Are you married?"

Okay, so I didn't really say that. What I said was, "Yes, it sounds great."

"The salary is forty thou a year."

Forty thousand dollars a year? For a newsletter that probably wouldn't take more than a week each month to put together? Yikes. I'd just died and gone to paycheck heaven!

Well, not quite, I reminded myself. I didn't have the job yet. Far from it.

"So," Andrew said, putting the palms of his hands on his desk, waiting for the show to begin. "Let's take a look at your writing samples, shall we?"

Fortunately, I'd done some freelance journalism in the past. Human interest stuff. Garden Clubs. Senior Water Aerobics at the Y. The annual Santa Monica Frisbee Olympics for Dogs. Not exactly Woodward and Bernstein. But then, the Union National *Tattler* wasn't exactly the *Washington Post,* so I was hoping I might have a shot at that forty thou.

Act confident, I told myself, as I opened my attache case. *You've got some fine work here. For all you know, he'll be fascinated by octogenarians in water fins.*

But when I reached into my attaché case, disaster struck. Something else popped out along with my sample book. Something beige and meshy and queen sized. Oh, God! It was my waist-nipper pantyhose! Lying smack dab in the middle of Andrew Ferguson's Mark Cross blotter! With the cotton crotch staring him right in the face.

So that's where Prozac hid it!

This had to be one of the Top Ten Most Humiliating Moments of my Life. Both of us sat there for what seemed like an eternity, staring at the damn thing. I wanted to do something, but I was paralyzed with shame.

Finally Andrew broke the silence. He smiled and said:

"Got anything in a fishnet?"

I grabbed the pantyhose and stuffed it back in my attaché case, turning instantly from mute to motormouth. "Oh, gee, this is so awkward. It's all Prozac's fault—"

"Prozac? Are you on medication?"

"No, Prozac's my cat. And she's mad at me because I came home with chimichanga on my breath and I put her on a diet and expected her to eat Healthy Haddock Entrails but I broke down and fed her Bumblebee but then this morning I made her go back on the diet and—"

I was babbling like an idiot, and I couldn't stop myself. Oh, well. What did it matter? That forty thou was long gone. I'd kissed the job good-bye the minute Andrew Ferguson locked eyeballs with my cotton crotch.

The rest of the meeting floated by in a mortified blur. I saw Andrew's lips moving but I barely heard a word he said. Something about calling me if they were interested. (Yeah, right.) Finally, he shook my hand good-bye and I stumbled out past Queen Elizabeth and down the elevator to the parking lot.

I drove home burning with shame. As much as I tried, I couldn't erase the image of Andrew smiling that crooked smile of his and asking me if I had anything in fishnet.

When I got home, I found Prozac lolling on the sofa, not a care in the world.

"You little ratfink!" I said, waving the pantyhose in her face. "I suppose you thought this was funny, huh?"

Mildly amusing.

She began licking her genitals, obviously quite proud of herself.

"Well, maybe you think it's funny, but I don't. I'll have you know I'm furious. Absolutely furious. Really, Pro. I mean it. I'm pissed."

I stalked off to the kitchen and began tossing her diet cat food into the trash.

"You want to be fat? Be fat! See if I care! Have a pizza. Some ice cream. Maybe a hot fudge sundae."

She stood at the kitchen door, wide-eyed, as I hurled cans of cat food across the room.

It's funny about Prozac. She knows when she's crossed the line. Whenever she sees I'm truly angry, she turns into the cuddly, loveable kitty of my dreams, leaping onto my lap, nuzzling her little pink nose under my chin, purring in contentment at the very sound of my voice.

All of which she proceeded to do. Suddenly she was Miss Congeniality. But I was having none of it. I was cool. I was aloof. I was unforgiving. No matter how wide her eyes got, no matter how much she purred, I remained indifferent to her charms.

I was merciless, all right.

In fact, that night when she jumped into bed with me and got on her back for a belly rub, I made her wait a whole thirty seconds before I gave her one.

Chapter 6

The following week was relatively uneventful. There was no news from my parents in Florida, and I assumed that no news was good news. Although with Daddy, that's always a risky assumption.

On the home front, work was deadly. My only job was a brochure for one of my regular clients, the Ackerman Awning Company (*Just a Shade Better*). Needless to say, I didn't hear a word from Andrew Ferguson, not after the Great Pantyhose Episode.

Oh, well. Maybe if I played my cards right, I'd land a job with one of the PMS Club's wealthy members. If I couldn't work for the Union National *Tattler,* maybe I could turn out a *Yummy News* bulletin for Marybeth.

The only true spark of excitement that week happened at—of all places—the Shalom Retirement Home. Once a week I teach a class there called "Writing Your Life Memoirs."

There's not really much teaching involved. It's mostly listening. Each week my elderly students come to class with their memories scratched out on lined paper. Some of them are written well. Some of them are stiff and awkward. But all are written from the heart, and I consider it a privilege to hear them.

The only fly in the Shalom ointment is Abe Goldman, the lone man in the group. Mr. Goldman is the kind of student every teacher dreads: loud, yakky, and opinionated. Worst of all, the old fart actually has a crush on me, constantly flashing me his Polygrip grin and asking me to go for moonlight strolls in the parking lot.

The night after my PMS meeting, I drove over to Shalom, and Mr. Goldman, as he always did, nabbed the seat next to mine at the head of the rec room conference table.

"Hi, cookie!" he grinned. "Look what I brought you!"

He reached into his pants pocket and took out a none too clean hanky.

Just what I wanted. Dried snot.

"Now where the heck is that thing?" he said, rummaging around his copious pants pocket. "Oh, here it is."

He pulled out a battered Puddin' Cup.

"I've been saving this for you all week. It's double fudge chocolate. I know how much you love chocolate."

It's true, I'm a confirmed chocoholic, but even I—a woman who almost named her cat Mallomar—was vaguely nauseated at the thought of eating a Puddin' Cup that had shared space with Mr. Goldman's dirty hanky all week.

"I brought you a spoon, too," he said, reaching into his pocket for a germ-ridden plastic spoon.

"Thanks," I gulped, as he shoved it toward me.

"So, cookie," he said. "How about it? You want to be my date for Mambo Mania?"

Every couple of months, Shalom hosted an event they called Mambo Mania. Which consisted mainly of elderly ladies dancing with each other (some of them on walkers) to Steve & Eydie singing *Besame Mucho*. Mr. Goldman always asked me to be his date for this gala affair, and I always said no.

"Sorry, Mr. Goldman, you know I don't dance."

"Who cares? We can always sneak out to the parking lot and neck."

Are you kidding? I'd rather eat this repulsive Puddin' Cup.

Ignoring his leer, I plastered a bright teachery smile on my face and asked, "Okay, class. Who wants to read first?"

Mr. Goldman's hand shot up. He always wanted to read first, one of his endless essays in the continuing saga of his life as a carpet salesman.

I looked around the room, desperate for another volunteer. I shot an encouraging look at Mrs. Pechter, a round powder puff of a woman with bosoms as big as throw pillows. But Mrs. Pechter just smiled benignly and popped a caramel in her mouth. I smiled at birdlike Mrs. Rubin, who quickly averted her gaze to her lap. My ladies were always shy at the beginning of class. It took them a while to warm up. I smiled at Mrs. Zahler and Mrs. Greenberg, but they, too, kept their lips zipped.

Finally, I could ignore Mr. Goldman's flapping hand no longer.

"Go ahead, Mr. Goldman," I sighed.

And he was off and running. Droning on about the time he sold four rooms of broadloom to Henry Kissinger (who sprang for extra padding, in case you're interested).

Eyelids began to droop as Mr. Goldman rambled on about the astute foreign policy advice he gave his good buddy "Hank." Some of the ladies were nodding off. And oh, how I envied them. I, being the teacher, had to force myself to keep my eyelids propped open.

But inevitably, as it always did during one of Mr. Goldman's recitations, my mind began to wander. I thought about my disastrous meeting at Union National Bank. What a shame. It would've been great to land that job. What a welcome break from Ackerman Awnings and Toiletmaster's Plunge-a-Thon Specials.

And then, of course, there was Andrew Ferguson. *Quel* doll. I remembered his crooked smile and the way his hair curled at the nape of his neck. I wondered what it would be like to run my fingers through those curls. And before I knew it I was lost in a reverie of me and Andrew in a hot tub drinking champagne and reminiscing over how we first met.

You know, he was telling me, as I ran my fingers through his curls, *I took one look at those waist-nipper pantyhose with the cotton crotch and right then and there I knew I had to have you—*

Oh, dear, no. That simply didn't work. No one in their right mind would be turned on by my industrial-strength pantyhose. I really had to work on my fantasy skills if I expected to have any sex life whatsoever.

It was then that I realized Mr. Goldman had stopped talking. He'd probably finished his essay, and I hadn't even noticed. I looked over at him, expecting to see him beaming with pride, the way he always did when he was through reading. But no, he just stood there staring at the doorway, his eyes bulging, his jaw gaping.

I followed his gaze, and my jaw did a little gaping of its own.

There in the doorway stood an eightysomething Las Vegas showgirl.

Okay, technically she wasn't dressed like a showgirl. She wasn't wearing pasties or a G-string or feathers in her hair. But she was wearing tight capri pants, towering wedgie heels, and a plunging spandex top that revealed a San Andreas–sized cleavage. Her eyelids were slathered with sparkly turquoise eyeshadow, her fingers were studded with honker cubic zirconia rings, and her copper-red hair was piled high on her head in a hurricane-proof beehive.

I'm guessing she was somewhere in her eighties, because that was the median age of Shalom residents, but it was hard to tell underneath her thick layer of make-up.

"Hiya!" she said, snapping some gum. "I'm Goldie. Goldie Marcus."

We all just sat there, staring at her. Even Mr. Goldman was at a loss for words.

"I just moved in today. From Paramus, New Jersey. My son took me out to dinner, so I didn't get a chance to meet anybody yet. Anyhow, they told me about the writing class, and I wanted to join."

I finally managed to jump-start my vocal chords. "Of course, Ms. Marcus. Take a seat."

"Here!" Mr. Goldman shouted. "Sit here! Next to me!"

He practically knocked poor Mrs. Rubin off her seat as he wedged in a chair by his side. Goldie Marcus tottered across the room on her wedgies and shot Mr. Goldman a seductive grin.

"Have a Puddin' Cup!"

And with that, Mr. Goldman grabbed the Puddin' Cup he'd given me earlier and slid it over to her. "It's double fudge chocolate."

The nerve of the bum! Giving her *my* Puddin' Cup. Yes, I know I said it was repulsive, but it was double fudge, after all. And I could have always sprayed the lid with Lysol when I got home.

"Thanks, hon."

Was it my imagination, or did I actually see Goldie wink at him?

"My pleasure, dear lady," he said, practically bowing. "My pleasure!"

"Welcome to our memoir-writing class, Ms. Marcus," I said.

"Please. Call me Goldie."

"Everybody, let's welcome Goldie to the class."

The other ladies exchanged sidelong glances of disapproval and murmured tepid hellos.

"Well, Goldie. Each week, we try to bring an essay to read. It doesn't have to be long," I said, shooting Mr. Goldman a meaningful look. "Just a page or two."

"Oh, I know all about the essays. Mrs. Maitland told me everything." Mrs. Maitland was Shalom's saint-cum-administrator. "I took lots of writing classes back in Paramus."

"That's wonderful," Mr. Goldman boomed, staring worshipfully in the general direction of her cleavage. "Taking classes is just wonderful!"

Goldie shot him another smile, followed by yet another wink.

Mrs. Pechter saw the wink and sniffed in disdain. Mrs. Rubin, who played Robin to Mrs. Pechter's Batman, sniffed, too, only not quite as loud as her more imposing friend.

"In fact," Goldie announced, "I brought something to read tonight." She rummaged through her purse and took out a piece of paper. "It got an A in my last writing class."

"An A!" Mr. Goldman boomed. "How about that? An A!"

"You're only supposed to read things you wrote for *this* class," Mrs. Pechter pouted. "Isn't that right, Jaine?"

"Well, yes," I said, "that's true. But as long as Goldie brought it, she might as well read it."

As far as I was concerned, anything that took the spotlight away from Mr. Goldman was okay with me.

"But Abe wasn't finished reading," Mrs. Pechter protested.

It had to be the first time in the history of the class that anyone ever asked to hear more of Mr. Goldman.

"Oh, I talked enough," Mr. Goldman said. "Time to give somebody else a chance."

Mr. Goldman giving somebody else a chance? Alert the media!

"Go on, Goldie," he urged.

She unfolded her piece of paper, which had obviously been in her purse for decades, just waiting to be whipped out, and began:

My Favorite Things, by Goldie Marcus.

It was a shameless ripoff of the Julie Andrews song from *The Sound of Music.* Instead of raindrops and snowflakes and whiskers on kittens, Goldie preferred rhinestones and lip gloss and herring in sour cream, preferably with a side of dill pickles.

With each Favorite Thing, Mr. Goldman let out an explosive burst of approval. "Me, too! I love that!"

The other ladies in the class looked at one another and rolled their eyes.

Goldie finished to a hostile silence. Normally the ladies applauded each other's essays in a show of sisterly support, but not that night.

The silence was finally broken by Mr. Goldman, who leapt to his feet and shouted: "Wonderful! Wonderful! Such terrific writing. Jackie Collins couldn't have done better."

"Very nice, Goldie," I managed to lie. "Although next time, it might be better to write about something that actually happened to you. That's what we try to do in a memoir-writing class. Now, who wants to read next?"

Mrs. Pechter raised her hand. "I've got an *essay*," she said. "Not a *list*."

And she proceeded to read about *My Most Unforgettable Character*. Sad to say, I've totally forgotten Mrs. Pechter's most unforgettable character. I wasn't concentrating. Nobody was. Not with Goldie Marcus in the room. All eyes were drawn to her as she sat there, fanning her impressive cleavage with her list of Favorite Things.

Finally, the last essay was read and it was time go.

The ladies gathered their back-support cushions and headed for the door, shooting covert glances at Goldie. Goldie, meanwhile, put her Puddin' Cup in her leopard-skin tote bag and smiled genially as Mr. Goldman volunteered to show her the ropes at Shalom.

The last thing I heard him say as they headed out together was, "Say, cookie. You like to mambo?"

I drove home, rattled by the effects of Hurricane Goldie. I wondered if my class would ever be the same again. Oh, well. Maybe with Goldie around, Mr. Goldman would finally learn some manners. I pictured the two of them together, going for moonlight strolls in the parking lot. What if they got married? Then Goldie would be Mrs. Goldie Goldman.

It was with these thoughts flitting around my brain that I climbed into bed and turned on the TV. I zapped aimlessly past ancient sitcom reruns, Ron Popeil infomercials, and sweaty bodies on the Whoopsie Doodle channel.

It was only when I happened to click on the Animal Channel that all thoughts of Goldie and Mr. Goldman vanished into the night.

They were showing a documentary about obesity in cats. I watched, horrified, as poor overweight cats struggled to breathe. A stern veterinarian lectured on the evils of feeding your cat human food. I gasped when they showed the deteriorated liver of a cat who was fed a steady diet of Chicken McNuggets, one of Prozac's favorite snacks. Finally, there was heartbreaking footage of a cat owner weeping at her kitty's grave.

"If only I'd put Taffy on a diet," she sobbed.

I watched as much as I could stand and then switched to a Lucy rerun. But even Lucy couldn't quell my panic, which by now was in full swing. If I cared about Prozac, I simply had to start feeding her diet food again.

I picked her up from where she was sprawled on my chest and cuddled her in my arms.

"You've got to go back on your diet, darling. It's for your own good. Do you want to wind up like poor Taffy?"

She wriggled out of my arms and shot me a baleful look.

Oh, don't believe everything you see on TV.

And with that, she jumped down from the bed and stalked off to the living room sofa. It looked like I'd be sleeping alone. But I didn't care. This time, I was going to hang tough. There'd be hell to pay, but I'd pay it.

What I didn't know at the time was that when it came to troubles looming ahead, Prozac's diet was just the tip of the iceberg.

YOU'VE GOT MAIL

To: Jausten
From: Shoptillyoudrop
Subject: Completely Bananas!

All I can say is—it's a good thing I ordered those Stress-Less pills. I've been gobbling them like Tic Tacs.

Your father has gone completely bananas. Yesterday during a shuffleboard game at the clubhouse, he actually plucked a hair from Reverend Sternmuller's head! He pretended he saw a bee on his hair and was swiping it away, but he later told me he pulled the hair on purpose to get a DNA sample. He sent it off to the FBI this morning.

And if that wasn't enough, today we were having lunch at Mimi's, a charming little restaurant in town, and who should be there but Reverend Sternmuller, having lunch with Greta Gustafson, who's been shamelessly throwing herself at the poor man. I swear, Greta has cooked more dinners in the past week than Swanson's.

Anyhow, the minute they left the restaurant, Daddy raced over to their table and took Reverend Sternmuller's fork!

"What on earth are you doing with that fork?" I asked him when he came back with the darn thing wrapped in a napkin.

"I'm going to send it to the FBI to check for fingerprints."

Then he put it in his pocket, along with several dinner rolls. It's bad enough that he insists on taking souvenir rolls from every restaurant in Florida, but to take a fork, too—well, I just about died.

And that was just the beginning. After we finished our lunch—your father insisted on ordering the bacon cheese-burger when Dr. May has told him a million times to watch his cholesterol—we were heading out the door when the manager stopped Daddy and accused him of stealing the fork. Which, technically, I suppose he was.

He and Daddy got into a big fight, and the next thing you know Kevin (that was the manager's name) wouldn't let us leave the restaurant until Daddy paid him ten dollars for the fork. By now, the whole restaurant was staring at us, and Daddy threatened to report Kevin to *America's Most Wanted,* but Kevin just laughed, and I was so humiliated I gave him the ten dollars and dragged Daddy outside with-out even getting one of their chocolate mints, which I really love.

Anyhow, I'm so mad, I could just spit.

Mom

To: Jausten
From: DaddyO

Hi, honeybunch—

I'm making lots of progress on the Hugo Boss case. Plus, I had a terrific cheeseburger for lunch today.

Your loving,
Daddy

Chapter 7

At 7 A.M. the next morning I was in the supermarket buying diet cat foot. At 7:30 Prozac was waving her tush in the air as she walked away from it.

I'd sprinkled a few kitty treats on top of the Lean 'N Lively Lamb Guts to lure her in. She ate the treats, careful not to ingest any of the offending lamb guts, then began howling for more treats.

"Sorry, Pro," I said, my voice steely with resolution. "For once, I am not weakening."

She continued howling while I made my instant coffee. Then, much to my surprise, she stopped. Usually, when she wants something she can keep up her wailing for hours on end.

But I guess this time she could tell I meant business, that I wasn't going to cave in. Interesting how effective a little discipline can be. I really had to start being stricter with her and assert my authority. If she got hungry enough, eventually she'd break down and eat her diet food. It was as simple as that.

So it was with a feeling of accomplishment that I dropped a Pop Tart in the toaster for my breakfast. Prozac let out an indignant meow.

You call that fair? You get to eat Pop Tarts, and I'm stuck with Lite 'N Lively Lamb Crud?

It was then that she stalked off to the living room, treating me to that scenic view of her tush.

I gobbled my Pop Tart standing up at the kitchen sink, safely out of Prozac's line of vision, then went to my office, otherwise known as my dining table, to check my e-mails.

Can you believe Daddy? Stealing a fork to get Reverend Sternmuller's fingerprints? And pulling a hair from his head for his DNA? It's just lucky he didn't try to get a blood sample.

But I couldn't sit around all day worrying about Daddy. That was Mom's job.

I spent the next hour or so fine-tuning the Ackerman Awning Brochure (*With Ackerman, You've Got It Made in the Shade!*), then got dressed and ran out to do some errands.

I was heading down the path to my Corolla when I bumped into my neighbor Lance.

"Hey, Jaine. How's it going?" he said, the sun glinting off his thick blond curls. Lance is a shoe salesman at Neiman Marcus, and he always dresses the part. He flicked a nonexistent speck of lint from his Ermenegildo Zegna suit. (No, Ermenegildo Zegna is not, as I once thought, a rare skin disease. It's a designer label, one of Lance's favorites.)

"I heard Prozac on the warpath this morning," he said. "Is she still on her diet?"

"Yes, she most definitely is."

"She lose any weight yet?"

"Well, no. She's putting up a bit of a fight. It's going to be a battle of wills between us, but trust me, I'm going to win."

"Nothing personal, hon. But my money's on the cat."

Then he waved good-bye and headed off to his Mini Cooper.

Well, phooey on him. I hoped his curls wilted in the smog. Really, it was most annoying how he just assumed I was incapable of putting my own cat on a diet. Well, I'd show him. Before long, Prozac would be svelte enough to lick her privates on the runways of Milan.

* * *

I got in my Corolla and was tooling off to the dry cleaners with a load of slacks and silk blouses in the backseat when I happened to pass a Goodwill store. On an impulse I decided to stop in. Sometimes I find some really neat stuff at thrift shops.

I'd pulled into the parking lot and was just getting out of my car when I saw someone familiar walking toward me from the drop-off area. It was Ashley, the big-boobed, margarita-toting gal from the PMS Club.

Suddenly I was embarrassed. I didn't want her to know that I shopped at Goodwill. I realized I was being ridiculous. I remembered how much fun Ashley had been at the club meeting, how down-to-earth. Not the least bit snobby. She wouldn't think less of me if I bought my clothes here. Why, lots of people think it's chic to shop at Goodwill. But for some insane reason, I was embarrassed. Maybe it was Ashley's silver Jaguar gleaming in the parking lot, or the multiple carats of diamonds studded in her ears.

I reached down into my Corolla, pretending to be looking for something, hoping she hadn't recognized me, but it was too late.

"Jaine? Is that you?"

I straightened up and smiled.

"Oh, hi, Ashley."

She hurried over, her ample boobs bouncing with each step.

"Jaine, sweetie. We're so happy you're joining the club."

"Me, too."

"You're coming to the meeting tonight, aren't you?" she asked.

"Of course."

She glanced in the backseat of my car and saw my dry cleaning.

"You dropping off a donation?"

"Why, yes," I said.

And then, to my horror, I realized I was opening the car door and gathering my clothes in my arms.

What the heck was I doing? Was I nuts? Why on earth hadn't I simply told her that I was shopping there? Oh, well. I'd just walk over with my dry cleaning and then wait till she was gone and put the stuff back in the car.

But that was not to be.

"I just dropped off a bunch of slacks that shrunk in my closet," Ashley said, laughing. "C'mon. I'll keep you company while you make your donation and we can gossip."

And so she walked me to the drop-off area, carrying on a stream of chatter that floated in and out of my consciousness:

"Can you believe Rochelle's empanadas with those Mexican flags? She's Martha Stewart channeling *Viva Zapata!* . . . Marybeth and I were best friends in college, but she can be a bit much with her yummy news. . . . Doris . . . what a hoot. I hope I'm half as feisty when I'm her age. . . . And Colin . . . why are the cute ones always gay?"

She went on and on and before I knew it, I was giving my dry cleaning to a Goodwill guy in a wheelchair.

"Don't forget to get a receipt," Ashley said. "Tax write-off, you know."

Yeah, right. First you need some income before you have to worry about taxes.

I took my receipt and watched in misery as my Ann Taylor silk blouses were tossed on top of somebody's old VCR.

"C'mon, hon," Ashley said, taking me by the arm, enveloping me in the heady aroma of her Vera Wang perfume. "You've done your good deed for the day."

We walked back to our respective cars, and at last she got into her Jag.

"See you tonight," she called out.

I waved feebly and watched as she drove off. The minute she was gone, I dashed back to the drop-off area.

The guy in the wheelchair, whose name tag said *Carlos*, looked up at me.

"Can I help you?"

"I'm sorry, but I'd like my clothes back."

Carlos's eyes widened with disbelief.

"You want to take back your donation?" His voice was a tad louder than I would have liked.

Several other workers gathered around.

"What's going on?" one of them asked.

"She wants to take back her donation."

"You don't understand; it wasn't really a donation. It was my dry cleaning."

Carlos shook his head, disgusted.

"Go ahead," he said, pointing to my clothes, which were still on top of the VCR, "take them back."

I felt the others shooting dagger looks at my back as I gathered my clothes.

"Why not take the VCR while you're at it?" Carlos muttered.

"It's people like her," another one said, "who give charity a bad name."

I slunk out, feeling like a cockroach in a five-star restaurant. It looked like I wouldn't be shopping at that Goodwill any time in the next millennium.

I finished the rest of my errands and drove home, certain that by now Prozac had caved in and eaten her diet food. Well, I was half right. She'd eaten. But not the diet food. I found her sprawled on the kitchen counter, like a drunk after a binge. Somehow she'd managed to claw the lid off her kitty treats and she'd scarfed down every last one of them.

She looked up at me with what I could swear was a smirk.

Score one for the furball.

Chapter 8

When Pam and I showed up at the PMS Club that night, I knew right away there was something wrong with Rochelle. She had a wild look in her eyes that hadn't been there the week before. Her limp hair had taken on a life of its own and stood out in angry spokes from her pony tail. She wore a T-shirt that seemed to match her mood. *I'm Out of Estrogen and I've Got a Gun* were the words emblazoned across her chest.

This week, instead of sporting a dishtowel slung over her shoulder, she greeted us at the door waving a margarita.

"Hi, there," she said, blowing a healthy blast of tequila in our direction.

Pam and I had dined al fresco at the Jack in the Box, where we were lucky enough to nab a table next to a colorful fellow reading Kafka and sipping rotgut whiskey through a straw.

We'd driven over to the PMS Club in my Corolla, and now we stood in Rochelle's foyer trying not to get too close to the tequila fumes.

"C'mon in, gals," she said. Only "gals" came out "galsh," her speech slurred from her trip to Margaritaville.

"Are you okay, Rochelle?" Pam asked.

"Fine!" she said, with a bitter laugh. "Never better."

She headed for the living room, almost tripping over an umbrella stand.

"Oopsie," she said, righting herself against the stairway banister. "Why don't you two go upstairs and see my new master bath?"

"It's finally finished?" Pam said.

"Yes." Rochelle's eyes narrowed into angry slits. "My dear friend Marybeth put the finishing touches on it today."

You didn't have to be a rocket scientist to notice the sarcasm dripping from the words *dear friend.*

"Damn," Rochelle said, sniffing. "The empanadas. I think I burnt 'em."

She lurched off to the kitchen, and Pam and I exchanged boggled looks.

"What's got into her?" Pam said.

"About a fifth of tequila," I guessed.

Pam shook her head, puzzled, then shrugged. "Well, come on. Let's go see the designer loo."

We headed upstairs to the master bath, which was a symphony of peach and sage—with his 'n hers sinks, marble countertops, a stall shower with about a gazillion jets, and a tub big enough to swim laps. There was even a separate room for the toilet. Or, as they call it in Brentwood, "the commode."

We found Colin bent over the commode, installing a roll of toilet paper.

"Would you believe I had to go to five different markets before I found this toilet paper?" he groused. "Marybeth insisted it had to match the towels exactly. For crying out loud, the towels are in a whole other room."

He got up, his jaw clenched in anger.

"Some day I'm gonna kill that bitch."

"And hello to you, too," Pam said.

He broke out in a grin.

"Hi, guys. Sorry to whine. What can I say? The woman is hell to work for. But I've got to look on the plus side, right? At least she underpays me.

"So what do you think?" he asked, gesturing around the bathroom.

"It's great," I said.

"Look at this linen closet." Colin opened a closet that ran a full wall's length.

Pam whistled softly. "The rich not only get richer; they get closet space, too."

"Well, I'm going downstairs," Colin said. "After my Great Toilet Paper Hunt, I need a margarita."

"Speaking of margaritas, what's with Rochelle?" Pam asked. "She's tanked already, and she hardly ever drinks."

"I don't know. She was fine when Marybeth and I were here earlier today. Her usual compulsive hostess self. Running around asking the plumbers if she could bring them some fresh-squeezed lemonade. But when I came back about a half-hour ago, she was sloshed."

"Maybe she finally cracked under the stress of remodeling," I suggested.

"Who knows?" Colin said. "All I know is I need that margarita. You gals coming?"

"Nah," Pam said. "I want to stay and snoop in their medicine cabinets."

"Rochelle's is boring," Colin said. "But check Marty's out."

With a weary wave, he headed back downstairs, and Pam began rummaging through the medicine cabinets.

"Pam, do you think we should be doing this?"

"Of course not. That's why it's so much fun."

Colin was right. There was nothing exciting in Rochelle's medicine cabinet. Just your run-of-the-mill over the counter cold meds. But when Pam opened Marty's, her eyes widened.

"Look at this," she said, taking out a prescription vial. "Viagra!"

I remembered what Rochelle had said about her husband, that he was cold and distant and coming home at all hours.

A cynical voice came from the doorway.

"Whoever he's using that stuff with sure as hell isn't Rochelle."

We turned to see Doris, the club's senior member.

How embarrassing. She'd obviously seen us snooping.

"Um . . . I had something stuck in my teeth," I stammered, "and we were just looking for some floss."

"Oh, please," Doris said, brushing away my lie. "We all snoop in other people's medicine cabinets. It's human nature."

She checked herself out in the mirror over the his 'n hers sinks.

"Great lighting. I don't look a day over fifty-nine."

Then she plopped herself down on the edge of the enormous tub.

"Poor Rochelle," she sighed. "I'm sure Marty's cheating on her. At least she can console herself with a nice jacuzzi bath." She looked around the room appraisingly. "What a palace. I wish I'd had his 'n hers sinks when I was married. You wouldn't believe the disgusting stuff my husband used to leave in the sink."

"I'd believe it," I said, remembering The Blob's delightful habit of leaving his toenail clippings in ours.

"Yep, this is some bathroom," Doris said. "If things go bad in the divorce she can always sublet it as an apartment."

"Do you really think they're headed for a divorce?" I asked.

"If she's lucky. Well," she said, hoisting herself up from

the tub, "I'd better go downstairs and help Rochelle out in the kitchen. Poor thing is three sheets to the wind."

"We'd better go, too," I said.

"We'll be right down," Pam said, grabbing me by the elbow. "Jaine has to take a tinkle first."

"Okay," Doris said. "See you down there."

When she was gone, I turned to Pam, puzzled.

"What was that all about? I don't have to take a tinkle."

"I know. But I want to sneak a peek at their bedroom. See if there are any mirrors over the bed."

"Pam! You're terrible." Then I grinned. "That's one of the reasons I like you so much."

We tiptoed out of the bathroom and were heading down the hallway in search of the master bedroom when we heard footsteps coming up the stairs.

"Yoo hoo! Pam! Jaine! You up there?"

It was Ashley. We scooted back toward the bathroom.

"Yeah, Ash," Pam called down. "We just saw the Taj Mahal. It's fab."

Ashley came up the steps, dressed to kill in a cashmere slack set that cost more than my car.

"Hi, honey," she said to me. "I found the most marvelous pair of shoes at Saks after I saw you today. What did you do? Something fun, I hope."

Sure, if you consider writing about awning rot fun.

"Just worked on a writing assignment."

"Let me see the heavenly can," Ashley said, marching over to the bathroom on her $500 shoes.

"Holy crap!" she said. "And I use the word *crap* advisedly. I'll bet the Good Lord himself doesn't go potty in a place this grand!"

Foiled by the appearance of Ashley, Pam and I abandoned our plan to snoop around Rochelle's bedroom and followed

Ashley back downstairs to the kitchen to see if Rochelle needed any help.

We found Colin pouring margaritas from the blender, and Doris at the kitchen sink, scraping the bottoms of Rochelle's empanadas, which were burnt to a crisp. Rochelle was sitting at her kitchen island, nursing a margarita, staring at the empanadas with glazed eyes.

"Aw, screw it," Rochelle said, getting up from her stool. She grabbed the empanadas from Doris and tossed them carelessly onto a serving plate. "So what if they're a little burnt? Makes 'em nice and crunchy."

I blinked, amazed. Was this the same perfectionist I saw running around like a wind-up toy last week?

"Here," she said to Doris, handing her the plate. "Bring 'em into the living room."

"What about the Mexican flags?" Doris asked.

"Who cares about the flags?" Rochelle said, taking another slug of her margarita. "They always were silly, weren't they?"

Suddenly tears welled in her eyes.

"I'm a silly woman," she said. "Always have been."

Then she lurched toward the living room.

The rest of us exchanged alarmed looks and hurried after her.

"Rochelle, honey," Ashley said, putting her arm around her, "what's wrong?"

"Nothing. Nothing at all. Everything's right as rain!" she said, with a sweeping gesture that almost knocked over a nearby floor lamp.

Ashley led her to a seat on the sectional. The rest of us took our seats awkwardly. Nobody said anything; we all just sat there, about as relaxed as a bunch of root canal patients.

I glanced down at the coffee table and saw that this week

there was no elaborate spread. No nuts. No pretzels. No tri-colored chips, salted and unsalted. Just the burnt empanadas.

It was at that moment that the doorbell rang.

"Oh," Rochelle said, her eyes narrowing. "That must be my dear friend Marybeth." Once again, there was nothing dear about the way she referred to Marybeth.

"Come innnn," she shouted out in an exaggerated singsong.

Seconds later, Marybeth came sweeping into the living room carrying a vase of exquisite silk dogwood flowers, her cheeks flushed with excitement.

"Rochelle, honey, look what I got for your bathroom. Won't they look just lovely on the counter?"

"Just lovely," Rochelle echoed, in that same singsong voice.

Marybeth shot her a look. Clearly something was wrong, but she chose to ignore it. Instead, she plastered a bright smile on her face.

"I'll go and put them upstairs. You want to come have a look-see with me?"

"No," Rochelle said, "I don't want to go have a look-see."

"Okeydoke," Marybeth said, her smile still firmly in place. "Then I'll just run up and do it myself."

The silence became even more uncomfortable as Marybeth headed up the stairs.

At last it was Rochelle who broke it.

"Damn," she said, "I forgot the guacamole."

"I'll get it!" Everyone jumped up at once, each of us eager to make a break for it.

"No," Rochelle barked, with unaccustomed authority. "Everybody sit down. I'll go."

She hauled herself up from the depths of the sofa and started for the kitchen.

The minute she was gone, we all started buzzing.

"What the hell is going on?" Ashley said.

"Maybe she's got her period." I threw out lamely.

"Oh, please," Pam said. "Nobody ever got their period that bad. Except possibly Lizzie Borden."

"She's pissed at Marybeth about something," Doris said.

"Yeah," Colin grinned. "Isn't it great? I hope she rips her to shreds."

"Maybe she doesn't like the bathroom," I suggested.

"No way," Pam said. "Rochelle loves everything Marybeth does. If Marybeth told Rochelle poop was pretty, she'd buy it and frame it."

"The old Rochelle," Colin corrected. "Something's changed."

Rochelle came out from the kitchen with the guacamole in a stainless steel mixing bowl. She hadn't bothered to transfer it to her fancy chips 'n dips serving piece. She dumped it on the coffee table, then carelessly ripped open a bag of chips.

"Dig in, gals," she said, stepping over the chips that had fallen on the carpet. "Sorry the guac's turned brown, but it's been sitting in the fridge since four o'clock this afternoon. Oh, well. Tough tacos."

And with that she plopped back down onto the sofa and went back to sucking on her margarita.

What with the atmosphere being so strained, nobody had much of an appetite.

Nobody except me.

I dug into the guacamole with gusto. But it wasn't nearly as nice as it had been last week. Not only was it brown on top, but it was missing all those giant chunks of avocado. It had been pureed in the blender too long, so it looked more like pea soup than guacamole. And it had a strange, greasy aftertaste.

Between the greasy brown guacamole and the burnt empanadas, I was glad Pam and I had stopped off at the Jack in the Box. I only wished I'd ordered extra cheese on my Jumbo Jack. I was just reaching for a handful of chips when Marybeth came sweeping back into the room.

"The dogwoods look super!" She beamed at Rochelle. "Just super. The perfect finishing touch."

Rochelle sat silently, her shoulders hunched, running her finger around the rim of her margarita glass.

By now the tension in the room was so thick you could cut it with a hacksaw. But Marybeth, still pretending everything was peachy keen, perched herself down next to Rochelle and announced:

"Guess what, everybody! I've got yummy news."

Rochelle looked up from her margarita glass.

"Screw your yummy news."

Marybeth's smile vanished.

"What?"

"You heard me," Rochelle said. "Screw your yummy news. We're all sick of your sunshine blather."

Marybeth could no longer pretend that nothing was wrong.

"Rochelle, what's got into you?"

"No, the question is, what's got into you, Marybeth? Or should I say, *who's* got into you?"

A faint blush crept into Marybeth's cheeks.

"Listen up, everybody," Rochelle said, taking a healthy slug of what had to be her fourth margarita. "I've got news. Big news. I was right about Marty. He *is* having an affair. I found this in his underwear drawer, right next to a package of condoms."

She pulled out a photo from the pocket of her sweatpants and tossed it onto the coffee table.

Ashley, who was sitting closest to it, picked it up and gasped.

"Holy Moses!" she said, and passed it around. It was a

color photo of Marybeth, sprawled out on what looked like a motel bed, wearing nothing but a smile and a pair of crotchless panties.

Now any decent human being would have had the grace to look ashamed. But not Marybeth. She just sat there with that infuriating smile on her face.

"It's true," she said, her chin raised in defiance. "Marty and I are in love. We've been seeing each other for months. We knew we were meant for each other from the day our eyes met over the heated towel racks.

"Poor Rochelle." She tried to put a comforting hand on Rochelle's knee, but Rochelle flicked it away. "Face it, honey. Your marriage was over way before I came along. Marty outgrew you years ago. If it hadn't been me, it would have been someone else."

She reached for the bowl of guacamole.

"You've got to look on the bright side, Rochelle. It's not the end of the world. It's the start of a whole new beginning. Remember. Today is the first day of the rest of your life!"

If she uttered one more cliché, Strunk and White would rise from their graves and throttle her.

"Would somebody pass me the chips?" she chirped.

Like an automaton, I passed her the chips.

We all watched, amazed, as, without a shred of remorse, she scooped a wad of guacamole onto a chip.

"Rochelle, sweetie. This is probably the best thing that ever happened to you."

Rochelle stared at her with glazed eyes.

"Drop dead," she said, her voice hard with fury.

"I know you don't really mean that. You'll forgive me in time. You'll dance at my wedding. You'll see."

Marybeth popped the chip in her mouth and chewed happily for a second. Then suddenly her fresh-scrubbed cheeks turned a most unbecoming shade of gray. The next thing we knew she was on the floor, writhing in pain.

"Peanuts," she gasped. "Somebody put peanuts in the guaca—"

But she never did get to finish her thought. Because by then she was dead.

So much for dancing at her wedding.

Chapter 9

We all stood there, frozen, staring at Marybeth, who for once had nothing positive to say. Then Rochelle started wailing at the top of her lungs. The angry Rochelle had vanished; the old Rochelle was back and scared half out of her mind.

"Oh, my God!" she cried. "Does anybody know CPR?"

Doris got down on her knees and felt for a pulse.

"It's too late for CPR. She's gone."

At which point we all joined Rochelle in her hysteria and started babbling.

Someone with her wits about her (it certainly wasn't me) called the police, and minutes later, we heard sirens screaming. In no time, the place was swarming with cops. They ushered us across the foyer into the dining room while they scurried around, taking pictures and bagging items for evidence.

From my seat at the dining table I saw one of the policemen pick up the X-rated photo of Marybeth from the coffee table. He nudged one of his fellow officers and showed it to him. How ironic, I thought. Not long ago, Marybeth was posing naked in a motel bed for Marty. Now she was posing dead for a bunch of cops, on a carpet she'd probably chosen herself.

The detective on the case, Lt. Luke Clemmons, was a

skinny guy with wire-rimmed glasses and a cowlick popping up from a bad haircut. He looked more like an encyclopedia salesman than a man who poked around dead bodies for a living.

He led a sobbing Rochelle back to the living room and sat her down in an armchair, a respectful distance away from the corpse. Then he took out a pad and pen from his pocket protector and began asking questions.

I strained to hear snippets of their conversation: *"Deathly allergic to peanuts. . . . She was fine before she ate the guacamole. . . . in my husband's underwear drawer, under a package of condoms."* After that tidbit, she broke out into a fresh batch of tears.

Soon after that I saw an officer approach the homicide detective.

"Sorry to interrupt you, Lieutenant," I heard him say, "but look what we found in the garbage."

With rubber gloves, he held up a bottle of peanut oil for the detective's inspection.

So that's how Marybeth was killed. Not with peanuts. But with peanut oil.

As the medics rolled in a gurney and a body bag, a trim blonde officer with her hair in a ponytail bustled into the dining room and wrote down our names and phone numbers. She told us we could go, but that we'd soon be wanted for questioning.

We headed out into the foyer and I could hear Rochelle telling the skinny detective, "I swear, Lieutenant, I didn't put the peanut oil in the guacamole. You've got to believe me!"

But I saw the way he looked at her, the way he checked out her T-shirt with its *I'm Out of Estrogen and I've Got a Gun* message. For the time being, at least, Rochelle had Prime Suspect stamped all over her.

"You've got to excuse me now," she said, running her fingers through her already wild hair. "I really must clean up my kitchen. It's a mess."

"Now's not the time to be worrying about your kitchen, ma'am," the detective said gently.

That was for sure. Now was the time, if I was not mistaken, to be calling her attorney.

Doris stayed behind to keep Rochelle company until her ratfink of a husband got home. "I'd like to punch his lights out," Doris hissed. "And I would if my arthritis wasn't acting up."

The rest of us headed outside, where the cool night air felt wonderful against my cheeks. The last thing I heard as I walked out the door was one of the cops saying, "They call themselves the PMS Club. Sure looked like one of them had a case of runaway hormones tonight."

Ashley, Colin, Pam and I started down the driveway to our cars.

"How do you like that?" Colin said. "After all those years of putting flags in her empanadas, Rochelle finally flipped out." He shook his head in disbelief. "What do you bet the cops arrest her? After all, Marybeth was boffing her husband. She had the perfect motive for murder."

She wasn't the only one who had a motive, I thought. Hadn't I overheard Colin saying that he wanted to "kill that bitch" for giving someone else the partnership he thought he deserved?

"It's so hard to believe," Ashley said. "Meek little Rochelle."

"Yeah," said Colin, "but you saw how angry she was tonight. It was like she was a different person."

"You're right," Ashley echoed. "A different person."

With deep sighs, we exchanged good nights, then got in our cars and drove our separate ways.

"I just can't picture Rochelle as a killer," I said to Pam, as we headed back to Hollywood in my Corolla.

"I know. But like Colin said, she was awfully angry tonight."

"Yes, but you saw how horrified she was afterward, when she realized Marybeth was dead."

"Do you think it's possible she killed her in an insane rage, then came to her senses when she realized what she'd done?"

"I guess it's possible," I conceded. "But I don't believe it."

"But if she didn't do it," Pam said, "who did?"

"Anyone who had access to the guacamole after she made it. She said she made it at four o'clock. And Marybeth was killed at about nine. That's five hours for someone to sneak into the kitchen and add the oil."

"Omigod!" Pam shrieked.

I slammed on my brakes and swerved to the side of the road.

"What's wrong?"

"I just realized," Pam gasped. "If it's not Rochelle, it's probably one of the other club members!"

"Interesting insight," I said, pulling back into traffic. "Not interesting enough to total my car. But interesting."

Pam continued, oblivious to my sarcasm. "I mean, everybody was wandering around, upstairs and downstairs, in and out of the bathroom. Any one of them could have wandered into the kitchen when Rochelle was out of the room."

"That's true," I said. "One of them could have done it. After all, nobody really liked Marybeth."

"But not enough to kill her," Pam said, shaking her head in disbelief.

"I'm not so sure about that."

I told her about Colin's angry cell phone conversation.

"He was really pissed at Marybeth for passing him over for that partnership. Not only that, he was at the house a whole half-hour before any of us got there. He said he came to do the toilet paper. But how long does it take to change a roll of toilet paper? He could've easily gone down and doctored the guacamole."

We rode in silence for a while. I was lost in thought, imagining Colin tiptoeing into the kitchen with a roll of quilted peach toilet paper in one hand and a bottle of peanut oil in the other, when Pam let out another piercing scream.

Once again, I slammed on my brakes, setting off an angry volley of honks from the cars behind me.

"What is it now?"

"I'm sorry, Jaine. But it suddenly occurred to me: What if the cops think you or I did it?" She bit her lip in dismay. "Damn. The last thing I need on my new resume is *murder suspect.*"

"Not to worry," I reminded her, as I started up the car again. "We were with each other the entire time. We both know we were nowhere near that guacamole. We'll swear to it on a stack of bibles."

She sat back with a sigh of relief. But that didn't last long. Seconds later, she let out another panicked squeal.

"Now what's wrong?" This time, I went right on driving.

"What if the cops think we're lying to give each other alibis?"

Now it was my turn to panic. Pam was right. The cops might think we were in cahoots. If for some reason Rochelle turned out to be in the clear, I could be a suspect in a murder case.

Just my luck to join the PMS Club the week before the murder.

Which just goes to prove that there's no such thing as a free margarita.

Chapter 10

The next morning, Marybeth's murder was splashed all over the news. Obviously some blabbermouth cop had leaked the story to the press.

The headline in the *L.A. Times* was the most sedate: INTERIOR DECORATOR MURDERED IN BRENTWOOD. But the TV news guys were having a field day. *The PMS Murder* was what most of them were calling it, with phrases like *Killer Guacamole* and *Homicidal Hormones* thrown in for added chuckles.

Thankfully none of the club members' names were mentioned. We were described only as "a group of wealthy Westside socialites."

"How do you like that, Pro?" I said to Prozac, who was sprawled out on the sofa, licking her privates. "Bet you didn't know you were living with a wealthy Westside socialite."

But Prozac didn't bother to look up. She'd been giving me the cold shoulder ever since I tried to feed her some low-cal liver for breakfast. She'd looked at it like I'd just dropped a turd on the floor and began wailing like a banshee. But I hung tough. And eventually she gave up and stalked off to the living room.

For once, I'd shown her who was boss. True, I wound up eating my breakfast in the bathroom, perched on the edge of the tub, afraid of the dagger looks I'd get if she saw me eating my bagel dripping with butter. But the point is, I didn't back down and feed her the Bumblebee tuna she was gunning for.

I was just tiptoeing back to the kitchen for another bagel when the phone rang. I picked it up warily, afraid that maybe an enterprising reporter had tracked me down for a statement about the murder.

"Ms. Austen?" An unfamiliar male voice came on the line. It was a reporter, all right.

"Who's calling, please?" I said, lowering my voice an octave, intending to tell him he'd reached the wrong number.

"It's Andrew Ferguson, from Union National Bank. Can I speak with Ms. Austen, please?"

Damn. Why did I have to lower my voice? Now he thought I was a guy. He probably thought I was married. Or living with a man—either that, or a very masculine woman. Not that it mattered what he thought. After my marriage to The Blob, I'd sworn off men forever, or at least until they invented one who remembered to leave the toilet seat down. But still, for some unaccountable reason, I didn't want Andrew to think I was taken.

"Right," I said, my voice still lowered. "I'll go get her."

I waited a few beats, then came back on the line in my normal voice.

"Hello, Mr. Ferguson." Then I called out, as if to someone else, "Thank you, sir, for fixing that leak!

"Sorry," I said, getting back on the line. "The plumber was here fixing a leak. That's who answered the phone. The plumber."

"Really?" Andrew asked, puzzled. "Do you always let plumbers answer your phone for you?"

"Oh, we're good friends. In fact, we've known each other for years. I wouldn't let anybody else near my drains."

"He's your friend, and you call him 'sir'?"

"Yes, that's short for Sirhan. Sirhan, the plumber. Fabulous guy."

Would somebody please shut me up???

"Well, the reason I'm calling," Andrew said, "is that I wanted you to come back for another interview."

He wanted me back! In spite of my cotton crotch on his desk!

"I'd like you to show your writing samples to our CFO. Do you think you could stop by around eleven?"

"Absolutely!"

"Just ask the receptionist to show you to Sam Weinstock's office."

After thanking him profusely, I hung up and did a little happy dance.

"Guess what, Pro? He wants me back for another interview! Even after your scurrilous pantyhose trick! So there, you evil spawn of the devil!"

I scooped her up in my arms and planted a big wet smacker on her nose.

Forget it. I'm still mad at you.

Then she wriggled free from my arms and jumped back on the sofa.

"Be that way. See if I care. You can sulk all you want, but you can't rain on my parade."

With that, I tootled off to the bathroom, where I wiped bagel crumbs from the bottom of the tub and ran a bath.

I sat in the tub for a good twenty minutes, up to my neck in strawberry-scented bath bubbles, dreaming of what I'd do if I got the job at Union National and was bringing home forty thou a year. I'd buy a new car, that was for sure. Maybe even put some money down on a condo. I'd upgrade my computer and treat myself to a decent haircut which would magically transform me into a striking beauty, which would make me utterly irresistible to Andrew Ferguson, and before long we'd be locking eyeballs over a hot Xerox machine.

I was right in the middle of an X-rated fantasy of me and Andrew on our honeymoon in Tahiti when I remembered

Marybeth's murder. And just like that, my bubble burst. For crying out loud, they'd never hire me once they found out I was a murder suspect. Banks tended to be fussy about stuff like that.

I hauled myself out of the tub, in a deep funk. But then, as I dried my hair, I began to look on the bright side. After all, I reminded myself, nobody in the media had mentioned my name. Andrew and Mr. Weinstock had no way of knowing I was involved with the PMS murder. And technically, I wasn't a suspect. The cops hadn't accused me of anything. All they'd said was that they wanted to question me. And maybe even that wouldn't come to pass. For all I knew, they'd already arrested Marybeth's murderer and I'd never hear from them again.

It was at that moment, just when I was wiggling into my pantyhose and feeling hopeful again, that the phone rang. I hobbled over to get it. Wouldn't you know? It was the police. They wanted me down at police headquarters for questioning later that afternoon.

Okay, big deal, I told myself when I hung up. Just because they wanted to ask me a few questions didn't make me a murder suspect. All it made me was a witness. I forced myself to be upbeat as I finished dressing and put on my make-up. At last I was ready for my interview. Bathed, blown dry, shaved, plucked, and Prada-ed.

I surveyed myself in the mirror. Not bad, not bad at all.

I checked my attaché case for any unwanted gifts from Prozac. Say, a hairball or a Tampax or some delightful eau de kitty piss. I breathed a sigh of relief to find nothing amiss. Then I grabbed my car keys and started for the door.

"Aren't you going to wish me luck?" I asked Prozac, who was still sprawled out on the sofa. "It would mean an awful lot to me. You know how much I love you."

Tell it to the tush.

And with that, she rolled over, showing me exactly where I could put my love.

I showed up at Union National, where Queen Elizabeth the receptionist greeted me with an icy smile and pointed me down a plushly carpeted hallway toward Sam Weinstock's office.

Now I don't know what you think of when you hear the name Sam Weinstock. I pictured a short, fat fellow with more hair in his ears than on his head.

Well, I pictured wrong.

For starters, Sam was short for Samantha. And far from being short, fat and bald, Sam was tall, slender and impossibly beautiful. Her finely chiseled features were straight out of a Clinique ad. Her gleaming auburn hair was parted in the center, a fringe of perfectly cut bangs framing her face. Not a single hair on that spectacular head dared to stray out of place.

She and Andrew were laughing about something when I poked my head in the door. It was an intimate laugh. Something about the way they looked at each other told me they were more than just coworkers.

"Jaine!" Andrew said, jumping up from where he'd been comfortably slouched on Sam's sofa.

"Come on in," he said, waving me inside. His hair, I couldn't help noticing, was still curling most seductively at the nape of his neck.

"I'd like you to meet our CFO, Samantha Weinstock."

"Everyone calls me Sam," the auburn-haired stunner said.

She stood to greet me, her hip bones protruding from her slim pencil skirt. I felt like a tugboat in comparison.

"Hi," I said, no doubt bowling her over with my conversational skills.

"Lovely to meet you," she said, shaking my hand. For such a tiny little thing, she had a surprisingly strong grip.

She looked me up and down, taking in my unruly curls and my drugstore make-up. Under her wilting gaze, my Prada pantsuit suddenly felt like one of Ethel Mertz's housedresses.

Obviously deciding I was no competition for Andrew's affections, she permitted herself a faint smile.

"Sit down, and let's have a look at your writing."

"I think you're going to be very impressed with what Jaine's going to show you," Andrew said, winking at me. "I know I was."

Was it my imagination or had he just made a sneaky allusion to my pantyhose?

"She's really an excellent writer," he added.

"I'll be the judge of that," Sam said, with a tight laugh. It was meant to be a joke, but we all knew she wasn't kidding.

I reached down into my attaché case. In spite of the fact that I'd checked it for booby traps, I was still nervous. Could Prozac somehow have managed to sneak in something that I'd overlooked? I took a deep breath and pulled out my sample book, saying a tiny prayer of thanks when no kitty turd tumbled out onto Sam's desk.

She looked through my writing samples slowly, not saying a word, turning the pages with all the enthusiasm of an undertaker.

Finally, when I was convinced she was about to send me packing, she slapped the book shut and said, "Nice work. Very nice indeed."

She liked it! She actually liked it! Did this mean she was going to offer me the job?

Apparently not. Not yet.

"I'd like to know a little more about your work history," she said. "Tell me about yourself, Jaine."

She folded her arms across her chest and sat back in her chair, waiting to be impressed.

"Well, I started out as a hooker, but then I hit hard times and had to take up writing."

Okay, so I didn't really say that. I didn't say anything. Because just then, Sam's secretary, another elderly aristocrat, came to the door and reminded Sam that she and Andrew were late for their lunch reservations.

"Damn," Sam said, checking her watch. "You know how crowded it gets at Simon's. If we don't get there, they may not save our table. Why don't you come with us, Jaine, and we can continue the interview there?"

"Fine," I said. I'd heard about Simon's. It was a hot new steak house, an expense account destination, where the three-inch thick sirloins cost as much as a midsized Hyundai.

I couldn't wait to wrap myself around one of those steaks. Medium rare. With a heaping side of thick-cut fries. I was salivating already.

We rode over in Andrew's car, a jet black BMW convertible. Up to then, I'd always thought guys who drove BMWs were arrogant jerks, but suddenly BMWs didn't seem so pretentious, after all. I was certain Andrew must have bought his for the expert German engineering, that he wasn't even thinking about using his car as a shallow status symbol. Come to think of it, hadn't I read somewhere that *Consumer Reports* actually liked the BMW? Why, for all I knew, Ralph Nader drove one.

Sam and Andrew sat up front, while I jammed myself into the tiny backseat, my knees poking uncomfortably into my chest.

Like most convertible owners in Los Angeles, Andrew had the top down to take full advantage of the invigorating southland smog. As the BMW tore along the streets, the wind turned my normally unruly mop into a Brillo patch. Needless to say, it didn't touch Sam's. It wouldn't dare. She got out of the car looking every bit as perfect as when she got in.

I, on the other hand, got out bearing an uncanny resemblance to the Bride of Frankenstein. I caught a glimpse of myself in the restaurant's plate glass window and choked back a gasp. It looked like my hair had been styled with a salad spinner.

The minute we were in the restaurant, I excused myself and dashed to the ladies room. I tried to tame down my curls, but it was hopeless. Finally, I gave up and headed back to the table. Oh, well. At least there was a steak at the end of the rainbow.

I joined Sam and Andrew, who were ensconced side by side in a plush leather booth. If she were sitting any closer, she would've been in his lap. I wondered if they, like Kandi and Steve, would soon be playing footsy under the table.

I slid in across from them, blushing as my slacks made a godawful squeaky noise against the leather.

"The steaks here are marvelous," Andrew said. "You've got to try one."

"Oh, Andy," Sam said. "Jaine's not going to order a steak. Not if she expects to keep her girlish figure."

Hey, if I didn't know any better, I'd have sworn that was a dig. And I *did* know better, and it *was* a dig.

"You men are so lucky. You can pack it away and it never shows, but not us. Right, Porky?"

Okay, she didn't really call me Porky, but after that girlish figure crack, I knew that's what she was thinking.

When the waiter showed up, Andrew ordered the top sirloin medium rare with fries. With all my heart and soul, I wanted to say, "I'll have that, too." But I couldn't, not with Sam having practically ordered me not to. So I ordered what Sam was having, the chopped salad.

"So," Sam said, when the waiter was gone, "tell us about yourself, Jaine."

I launched into my spiel, telling her how I'd worked for years as an advertising copywriter before striking out on my own as a freelance writer, how I enjoyed the challenges of varied accounts and the satisfaction that comes from a job well done, all the while trying not to use the word *Toilet-masters* too much.

Finally, when I'd finished my tap dance, our lunch showed up. Andrew's steak was sizzling on the plate, a pat of butter melting on top. His thick-cut fries were golden brown and glistening with crystals of salt. It was all I could do to keep myself from reaching over and grabbing one.

I looked down at my chopped salad and cursed the day God ever invented lettuce.

I had no idea what we talked about during lunch. I was too busy watching as Andrew demolished his steak, piece by succulent piece. Oh, Lord, this was torture. At one point, a bit of ketchup from his fries landed on his chin. I swear, I almost leaned across the table and licked it off.

Then suddenly I realized Andrew was talking to me.

"What's that?" I said.

"Are you sure you've had enough to eat?" he asked, looking down at my plate.

I followed his gaze and saw to my amazement that I'd picked my plate clean. Somehow, I'd managed to shovel down every last shard of my salad.

"Oh, yes. I'm stuffed," I said, my stomach rumbling with hunger. "I couldn't eat another bite."

"Of course," he said, nodding solemnly. Was it my imagination, or was that a smile I saw lurking at the corners of his mouth?

Eventually, having barely touched half her salad, Sam proclaimed herself full.

"We don't want dessert, do we?" she asked.

"Hell, yes!" were the words I wish I'd been brave enough to utter. Instead, I just shook my head no as Sam signaled the waiter for the check.

"So, Jaine," she said, turning back to me. "Would you like to be editor of the Union National *Tattler*?"

Was this a trick question? If I said yes, would she say, *Haha. Fooled ya. You can't have it!*?

"Yes, I would," I took a chance and assured her.

"Well, then," she said, with a stiff smile, "the job is yours."

"Congratulations!" Andrew beamed. "Welcome aboard. When can you start?"

"As soon as you like."

"Great. I'll call you tomorrow and set up a meeting with the branch managers."

Sam settled the bill and we headed out to the parking lot. I was practically walking on air. Forgotten was my ghastly chopped salad; the only green I saw now were the paychecks heading my way.

The three of us stood in the parking lot, making idle chat while the valet got Andrew's BMW. Then, out of the corner of my eye, I saw Sam slip her hand into Andrew's pants pocket. It was a subtle gesture, but I got the distinct impression that she wanted me to see it, like a cat marking her territory.

When he realized he had more in his pocket than his spare change, Andrew flushed and shot Sam a shy smile.

Obviously Sam Weinstock was living out my bathtub fantasies.

I picked up my Corolla from the Union National parking lot and headed home, ravenous. There hadn't been enough food in that salad to keep an anorexic rabbit alive.

I almost felt like driving back to the restaurant and ordering a steak. But I didn't have a paycheck in my hot little hand yet, I reminded myself. So instead, I stopped off at the first eatery that I came across, a bastion of haute cuisine called Tommy's Taco Stand.

I ordered the beef burrito and a Coke, and I practically jumped over the counter to fix it, I was that hungry.

As I waited what seemed like an agonizingly long time for

the guy behind the counter to get my food, my mind kept drifting back to the sight of Sam's hand sliding into Andrew's pocket. I know I should've been doing cartwheels of joy about my new job, but all I could think of was Sam sitting with Andrew in *my* fantasy house in Malibu in *my* fantasy hot tub with *my* fantasy strawberries dipped in chocolate.

At last, my burrito came, and I tore into it like the starving woman that I was. I didn't even bother to take a seat at Tommy's outdoor wooden picnic table. I just stood at the curb gobbling down the burrito at the speed of light.

So there I was, my mouth full to capacity, burrito grease dribbling down my chin, when I happened to glance up at the cars at the stoplight. Suddenly the burrito turned to cement in my mouth. There, sitting at the light in his black BMW convertible, watching in disbelief as I stuffed my face, was Andrew Ferguson.

Then the light turned green, and he sped away.

It's at times like this that you have to look on the bright side. I mean, some day, when I'm in my eighties and taking a memoir-writing class, at least I'll have something to write about when the teacher asks us for an essay on "My Most Humiliating Moment."

Chapter 11

An hour later, I was sitting across from Lt. Luke Clemmons, trying not to stare at his cowlick and the way it jutted out from his scalp like a hairy question mark.

I finally managed to avert my gaze to his desk. It was immaculate. Not a hint of clutter anywhere. The papers in his In Box were precisely stacked, as if they they'd just come out of their wrapper. His stapler sat on his desk in perfect alignment with his paper clips, his pencil sharpener, and a mug of freshly sharpened pencils.

Clearly, the good lieutenant had a bit of an obsessive-compulsive disorder.

"Thank you for coming, Ms. Austen," he said, moving his stapler a millimeter to the right. "I just want to ask you a few questions."

"Of course."

"No need to be nervous."

Actually, I wasn't feeling the least bit nervous. I was still too busy feeling humiliated over my burrito fiasco with Andrew Ferguson.

"I wanted to talk to you first," he said, "before I saw the other club members."

"Oh?" I said, preening.

He must have heard about all the murders I've helped solve—murders you can read all about in *This Pen for Hire*,

Last Writes, Killer Blonde, and *Shoes to Die For,* now available in paperback wherever fine books are sold. (Forgive the shameless plugs, but if I don't toot my own horn, who will?)

"Oh, so you've heard about me."

He blinked, puzzled.

"No, can't say I have. Why would I have heard about you?"

"I've helped the police in several murder investigations."

"Are you a private detective? According to my notes, it says you're a writer."

"I'm a detective on the side."

"You have a license?"

"Well, no. Not actually."

His brow furrowed in concern.

"You can't be a P.I. without a license."

Now I *was* nervous.

"It's all very informal," I stammered. "I mean, it's not a real business. I just help people out."

"It better not be a business," he said, adjusting the already perfect lineup of his stapler, pencil sharpener and pencil mug. "That's a violation of Code 286297B."

"I promise," I said, sweat beginning to form on my brow, "it's not a real business."

"Well, all right," he said grudgingly. "Now let's get down to the matter at hand."

"Do you mind if I ask you something first, Lieutenant?"

"What is it?" There was more than a hint of impatience in his voice.

"I was just wondering. If you haven't heard about me, why did you want to see me before the others?"

"Because your last name begins with *A.* And I always conduct my interviews alphabetically."

Wow. The guy probably color coded his socks.

"*Now* can we get started?" He took out a tape recorder

from his desk and clicked it on. "Be sure to speak loudly and clearly."

I felt like I was back in sixth grade, in Ms. Martin's Public Speaking class.

Then he took out a steno pad and reached for one of his pencils.

"You're going to tape me *and* take notes, too?"

He nodded crisply. "Better safe than sorry."

Quick. Somebody send this guy to Fussbudgets Anonymous.

"So," he asked, sharpening his already sharp pencil. "How well did you know the deceased?"

"Not well at all. I just met her two weeks ago, when I joined the club."

"Were you fond of her?"

"To be perfectly honest, no."

"Why not?"

"Because she was an egotistical, cloying jerk."

I didn't actually put it like that. I figured I'd be a bit more discreet. What I said was, "She seemed a bit self-centered and insensitive."

He nodded, taking notes as I talked. I bet he dotted every damn one of his i's.

"I don't think anybody in the club really liked Marybeth," I said. "Except for Rochelle. Until she found out about Marybeth's affair with her husband. Then, of course, she got angry. But really, Lieutenant, I can't believe Rochelle is capable of murder."

Clemmons looked up from his notes.

"Why don't you let us be the judge of that, Ms. Austen?" he said, plunging his pencil into his sharpener. For crying out loud, he'd been writing for all of thirty seconds; it couldn't possibly have needed sharpening.

"Can you think of anyone else in the club who might have had a motive to kill Marybeth?"

I hesitated to get Colin in trouble with the police, but I felt like I had no alternative. I told him how angry Colin had been at Marybeth for passing him over for a promotion.

"He said he wanted to kill her. It's hard to believe he really meant it. But he was at Rochelle's house a full half-hour before the rest of us got there. I can't help wondering if he had time to sneak down to the kitchen when Rochelle wasn't around and add the peanut oil to the guacamole."

Once again, Clemmons looked up sharply from his notes.

"How did you know about the peanut oil?"

"I saw one of the police officers show you the bottle. And I figured it out."

Clemmons scowled. He clearly didn't like me figuring things out.

"What about the others? Did you see anyone go into the kitchen alone that night?"

"No, we were all wandering around, looking at Rochelle's new bathroom. It was hard to keep track of who went where. I suppose any of them could have slipped into the kitchen. Except Pam Kenton, of course. She and I were together the whole evening."

Clemmons smiled a smile that oozed cynicism.

"Oh? How convenient for both of you."

Damn. Pam was right. He thought we were covering for each other.

"I can assure you, Lieutenant, neither of us went anywhere near that guacamole."

"Right," he said, snapping his steno pad shut. "Thank you for your time, Ms. Austen. I've got all I need to know. For now, anyway. Please notify us if you plan to leave town."

Ouch. I didn't like the sound of that.

"You know the way out."

I got up to go. I would've given anything to reach over and mess the papers in his In Box, but you know what a wuss I am. Instead, I used my purse to push his stapler an inch out of place.

It wasn't much, but it made me feel better.

I wasn't looking forward to my class at Shalom that night. I was certain the PMS Murder would be the topic du jour. Many of my students are news junkies. These are, after all, ladies of leisure with many hours to fill between bagels and bingo, and most of them while away the hours with Eyewitness News blasting in their rooms at full throttle. I fully expected them to be chattering about Marybeth's dramatic death by guacamole.

But I needn't have worried. When I showed up at Shalom's rec room, nobody was talking about the murder. They were preoccupied by another hot topic of discussion.

"I thought he was an idiot before," Mrs. Pechter was saying, "but now, he's worse than ever."

The others tsk tsked in agreement.

"Making such a fool of himself," Mrs. Rubin chirped.

"His wife is probably rolling over in her grave," Mrs. Zahler opined.

It didn't take a rocket scientist to figure out who they were talking about. It had to be Mr. Goldman. There were few other men living at Shalom. And none, I imagined, capable of provoking such ire.

Strange, I thought, that Mr. Goldman wasn't there yet. He was always in class when I showed up, always in the seat next to mine, waiting for me with a stale cupcake, wilted flower, or other exotic love offering. But tonight, Mr. Goldman was nowhere in sight. And neither was our recent arrival from Paramus, New Jersey, the flamboyant Goldie Marcus.

"Good evening, ladies," I said, settling down in my seat.

"Hello, Jaine, dolling," Mrs. Pechter said, leading a chorus of hellos.

"That poor dead wife of his," Mrs. Zahler resumed when they were through greeting me. "Can you imagine being married to a jerk like Abe?"

The others shook their heads. Nope, it was beyond their imaginations. And mine, too, if you must know.

"Jaine, you won't believe what's happened," Mrs. Pechter said, setting off a fresh round of tsks.

"It's disgusting," said Mrs. Greenberg.

"Makes me want to throw up," said Mrs. Fine.

"What?" I asked. "What's happened?"

But before anyone could answer, I found out for myself. Because just then Mr. Goldman walked into the room arm in arm with Goldie Marcus. Goldie hadn't changed since the last time I saw her. She was still an octogenarian pistol in leopard print capri pants and pink angora sweater, her orange hair piled on top of her head in an Aqua Net beehive.

But Mr. Goldman—holy mackerel! I couldn't believe my eyes. Gone was his gravy-stained cardigan and baggy pants. Tonight he wore a bright yellow and black checkered sports coat, about as subtle as a taxi cab, with white slacks and white loafers. He looked like a pimp on high blood pressure medication.

But that wasn't all. He'd dyed his three remaining strands of hair jet black. And as the pièce de résistance, he'd started to grow a mustache. Of course, after only a week, it was just stubble. But this, too, had been dyed black. So it looked like a smudge of charcoal on his upper lip.

A ripple of disapproval followed as he and Goldie headed for the two seats next to mine.

Now, I thought he looked ridiculous. And the ladies thought he looked ridiculous. But clearly Goldie Marcus did not share our opinion. She strutted across the room with her arm hooked in his, shooting him sexy come-hither smiles en route.

Mr. Goldman pulled out a chair for her with a flourish.

This from a man who'd been known to shove aside women in walkers to get first in line for the Belgian waffles at Sunday brunch.

"Look at him," I heard Mrs. Pechter mutter. "Sir Galahad."

The other ladies giggled.

Mr. Goldman glared at them, then turned to his lady love and beamed.

"Wanna kiss, doll?"

"You bet, Abie."

And with that, Mr. Goldman took out a Hershey's Kiss from his pocket and peeled off the foil. Then he popped it into Goldie's open mouth.

"Feh." Mrs. Pechter rolled her eyes in disgust.

"Don't mind Pechter," Mr. Goldman said to Goldie. "She's got no manners."

"Look who's talking," Mrs. Pechter said. "You're the one who uses your dentures as a bookmark."

"I only did that once!" Mr. Goldman protested. "Or twice."

"Okay, class," I said, sensing hostilities mounting. "Who wants to read first?"

"Me!" Goldie said, her hand shooting up in the air, cubic zirconia rings flashing.

"Go right ahead, Goldie." I smiled what I hoped was an encouraging smile.

She reached into her leopard-skin tote bag and pulled out a piece of paper. "I wrote it specially for this class." She beamed with pride.

"Very good," I nodded.

She cleared her throat and began to read.

My Favorite Things, Part II, by Goldie Marcus.

Obviously my request to write about a personal experience had fallen on deaf ears.

"What a terrific title!" Mr. Goldman gushed.

"It's not exactly a memoir," I said, "but go ahead."

And so Goldie told us about more of her favorite things, some of which were *Turquoise eyeshadow and long false eyelashes* and *Men with dark hair and sexy mustaches*.

Aha. So that's where Mr. Goldman's dyed hair and mustache came from.

When Goldie was through plagiarizing *The Sound of Music*, Mr. Goldman burst into applause.

"Bravo! Bravo! An A-plus! Right, Jaine?"

They both looked at me, eager for praise.

"It's very nice, Mrs. Marcus. But I'd really like you to try writing about an actual memory. That's what we do in a memoir-writing class."

"Of course," Mrs. Pechter muttered. "You're supposed to write about memories, not mustaches."

"Okay," I said, "who's next?"

Several of the ladies raised their hands but before I could call on any of them, Mr. Goldman said, "I'll go," and was up on his feet reading.

A Gal from Paramus, by Abe Goldman, he began, with a wink at his beloved.

> *There once was a gal from Paramus*
> *Who was beautiful, charming and glamorous*
> *The first time I saw her*
> *I had to adore her*
> *And that's why my heart is so amorous*

Then he bowed deeply from the waist and sat down.

"Oh, Abie, that's bee-u-ti-ful," was Goldie's glowing assessment of his talents.

Alas, she was alone in her praise.

"For crying out loud, Abe," Mrs. Pechter sneered. "This isn't a poetry class."

"That wasn't a poem," he sneered right back. "It was a limerick."

"Limerick, shmimerick. It doesn't belong in this class. Right, Jaine?"

"Actually, Mrs. Pechter has a point. From now on, I want only memoirs. And only read when I call on you, Mr. Goldman."

"Not only that," Mrs. Rubin piped up, "it didn't rhyme right."

Mr. Goldman managed to pry his eyes off Goldie and glared at Mrs. Rubin.

"Whaddaya mean, it didn't rhyme right?"

Mrs. Rubin wilted slightly under his glare but held her own.

"Paramus," she said firmly, "does not rhyme with glamorous."

"Or amorous," Mrs. Zahler added.

"Sure it does," said Mr. Goldman. "Paramus. Glam'rus. Am'rus."

The others groaned.

"I've got two words for you," Mrs. Pechter said. "Im Possible."

"Okay, class," I said, beginning to feel, as I so often do at Shalom, like a Madison Square Garden referee, "who wants to read next?"

I spent the rest of the class listening to proper essays. About trips to Hawaii; beloved relatives; and, from Mrs. Fine, *The Time My Daughter-in-Law Set Fire to Her Kitchen. Don't Ask.*

But truth be told, I was only half listening. I simply couldn't take my eyes off the lovebirds. As much as I tried not to, my eyes kept darting to Mr. Goldman, with that ridiculous mustache of his, peeling the tin foil off Hershey's Kisses for his Glam'rus Gal from Paramus.

When I got home from Shalom, I found five messages on my answering machine from the *L.A. Times*, wanting to interview me for a story they were writing. I pressed the erase button and bleeped them into oblivion. No way was I talking to the press.

Then I wandered into the kitchen to get myself an apple (okay, an Eskimo Pie). I was about to open the freezer when I looked down at Prozac's food bowl and gasped in surprise. The little angel had actually finished her Lite 'N Lively Liver Tidbits! Every last one of them!

I raced into the dining nook, where she was dozing on my computer keyboard.

"Oh, Prozac, honey," I cooed, scooping her up in my arms, "I'm so proud of you."

She was so thrilled to hear it, she almost stopped yawning.

See? I knew if I hung tough with her, she'd eventually weaken. And everyone said she had me wrapped around her little paw. What did they know, huh? I was a lot tougher than people gave me credit for.

Then I grabbed my Eskimo Pie and tiptoed off to the bathroom, hoping Prozac wouldn't hear the wrapper crinkle when I pulled it off.

YOU'VE GOT MAIL

To: Jausten
From: Shoptillyoudrop
Subject: Can't Show My Face

Oh, Lord! I can barely show my face in Tampa Vistas. You know how fast news travels around here. Everyone, just everyone, is talking about how Daddy stole a fork from Mimi's restaurant.

And if that weren't bad enough, Daddy actually went out and bought a listening device to spy on poor Reverend Sternmuller! A silly piece of junk called the "I-SpyMaster." He paid $69.95 for that thing and all it is is a headset they rent out at movies for people who are hard of hearing.

I told him if he used it in public I'd never speak to him again, but did that stop him? Noooo. He marched right over to the clubhouse with the "I-SpyMaster" on his head and plunked himself down a couple of tables away from Reverend Sternmuller. He pretended that the SpyMaster was an ordinary headset and that he was listening to his Walkman. But really he was shamelessly eavesdropping. Although why he expected Reverend Sternmuller to confess to being the Hugo Boss Strangler while playing backgammon with Greta Gustafson and Emmy Pearson, I'll never know.

It turns out all he heard was static, and it served him right.

Thank heavens for my Stress-Less pills. I don't know what I'd do without them, although I must admit they seem to be far more effective when I take them with a glass of sherry.

Your loving,
Mom

P.S. By the way, Reverend Sternmuller and Greta Gustafson are quite an item. People say wedding bells may be ringing any day now.

To: Jausten
From: DaddyO
Subject: Under Surveillance

I had Reverend Sternmuller, aka The Hugo Boss Strangler, under surveillance today, using a sophisticated listening device. But unfortunately, I didn't have much luck. The Strangler probably had an even more sophisticated blocking device that created a wall of static around him.

But don't worry, lambchop. I'll catch him sooner or later. Just you wait.

Your persevering,
Daddy

To: Jausten
From: Shoptillyoudrop
Subject: Bingo

Tonight's Bingo Night at the clubhouse. I hate to miss all the excitement (last week I won twelve dollars!), but I'm sure all the tongues will be wagging about Daddy.

I guess I'll have to stay home. But if I do, I'll only sit and stew and get more upset. And besides, why should I let Daddy's moronic behavior keep me from enjoying a perfectly lovely evening?

No, on second thought, I'm going! I'll just pop another Stress-Less pill and wash it down with an itsy bitsy glass of sherry. That should get me through the night.

To: Jausten
From: DaddyO

Your mom just left for bingo. I told her I was staying home because I had a headache. And she fell for it!

What a perfect opportunity to spin my web and trap the Hugo Boss Strangler. Yes, sweet pea, it's time for The Nose to spring into action!

Chapter 12

I shuddered when I checked my e-mails the next morning. Lord only knew what mischief "The Nose" was up to. Really, sometimes I think Daddy shouldn't be let outside without a leash.

Back on the home front, Prozac continued to be a good little Weight Watcher and dug into her Lite 'N Lively Liver Tidbits with gusto.

"Oh, sweetie," I gushed as she hunkered over her bowl, "I'm so proud of you."

I considered celebrating my victory in the battle of wills with a nice big plate of bacon and eggs and a toasted English muffin dripping with butter but decided against it. For one thing, I didn't think Prozac would appreciate my pigging out on bacon and eggs when she was stuck with her Lite 'N Lively liver glop. And for another thing, I didn't have any bacon. Or eggs. Or English muffins. Or butter, for that matter. A quick survey of my refrigerator yielded little more than a chunk of moldy Swiss cheese and jar of martini olives.

So I nuked myself some instant coffee and settled down with the morning paper.

I took one look at the front page and gasped in dismay. There, smiling out at me from under the headline PMS MURDER VICTIM, was a picture of Marybeth Olson, taken in the days when she was alive and well and driving everybody crazy.

But it was what was underneath Marybeth's picture that set my heart pounding. Yes, lined up beneath the unnerving caption AT THE SCENE OF THE CRIME were snapshots of the six remaining PMS Club members: Pam, Doris, Ashley, Rochelle, Colin, and yours truly, Jaine Austen.

There I was plastered on the front page of the *L.A. Times*—a murder suspect. Even more horrifying, they'd used my driver's license photo. The one where I looked like an extra from *Dawn of the Dead*. (If only I'd returned their calls last night, maybe I could have dashed over with a decent picture.)

I looked down at that awful picture and groaned. I looked like a poster girl for schizophrenia. If a jury had to convict one of us by looks alone, I'd be doing time in the pokey before the afternoon was out.

By now, I was in an advanced state of panic. What if the police thought I was the killer? What if they arrested me? And worst of all, what if my parents saw the paper? They'd be on the first plane out here—moving into my apartment, putting crocheted covers on my Kleenex boxes, and making me wear my retainer at night!

And just like that, I couldn't breathe. Yikes. I was hyperventilating. I had to force myself to calm down. I told myself to take deep breaths, but I couldn't suck in the air.

What was it that you were supposed to do when you're hyperventilating? Breathe into a paper bag! That's it. I raced around my apartment looking for a paper bag, but all I could find was a Bloomingdale's shopping bag. So there I was, trying to breathe into a Bloomingdale's Medium Brown Bag when the phone rang.

What if it was my parents? For a minute I considered letting the machine get it. But then I figured they couldn't possibly have seen the paper, not this quickly. And besides, I could ask whoever it was to call the paramedics and get me some oxygen.

Thank heavens, it was Kandi. I started breathing again at the sound of her voice.

"Oh, honey," she said. "I just saw the paper. It's awful."

"I know."

"I can't believe they used that hideous picture of you. You ought to write an angry letter to the editor."

"Kandi, I think you're losing sight of the important issue here. I'm a suspect in a murder case."

"Oh, foo. You couldn't possibly have killed anyone. Anybody who knows you knows what a sweetie you are."

"Unfortunately," I pointed out, "the police don't know me very well."

"And I never knew you had PMS," Kandi said, oblivious to my fears. "Why didn't you tell me?"

"But I don't actually have—"

"I could've sent you to my gynecologist, Dr. Sobol. All the celebrities use her. She's the Hormone Doctor to the Stars."

"Honey, I don't have PMS. The PMS Club is a women's support group. I had the bad luck to join two weeks before the murder."

"You poor thing. This just isn't our day, is it? You'll never guess what happened to me this morning. We found out that the actor who plays Ernie the Earwig fell out of his son's bunk bed while having sex with the babysitter. Anyhow, he broke one of his vertebrae and he's going to be in traction for the next month and now we've got to write him out of the next ten scripts. I'll be here till midnight for sure. And today's the day Steve and I were supposed to meet with Armando and choose a band for the wedding. Oh, well. They'll just have to choose one without me." She finally paused to take a breath. "But I can't believe I'm rambling on about my petty problems when you're in such a fix."

Frankly, neither could I.

"Jaine, honey. If you need an attorney, don't you worry. I'll pay for it. And if you want to stay at my apartment, you come right over. I'll hold your hand and make you hot cocoa with marshmallows, just the way you like it."

See? Just when you think Kandi is the most self-centered woman in the universe, she turns around and offers you her heart and her marshmallows. That's why we've been best friends all these years.

"Thanks, Kandi," I said with false bravado. "But I'll be okay."

The minute I hung up, the phone rang again.

What if, this time, it was my parents? What if the wire services picked up the story and they'd heard about the murder?

Gingerly I picked up the receiver.

But it wasn't my parents. It was worse. Much worse. It was Andrew Ferguson.

"I just saw the paper," he said solemnly.

My heart sank; I knew what was coming next.

"Sam and I talked it over, and I'm afraid that as long as your name is connected with a murder, we can't hire you."

"I understand," I managed to say.

"I'm really sorry, Jaine."

That made two of us.

I hung up and slumped down onto the sofa. From her perch on top of my computer keyboard Prozac saw how miserable I was and came rushing to my side. (Okay, so she didn't technically come rushing to my side. Technically, she went right on licking her privates, but I could tell she was worried about me.)

"Oh, Prozac," I moaned, "this is awful."

Not only had I lost the job, but Andrew Ferguson had seen my driver's license photo. That, on top of the Pantyhose-on-the-Desk Affair and the Stuffing-My-Face-with-Burrito Episode—it was all too horrible to contemplate.

Minutes later, the phone rang yet again. I picked it up listlessly, certain it was my parents. Oh, well. Who cared if they moved in with me and made me wear my retainer for the rest of my life? I'd totally lost the will to live.

But it was Andrew again.

"Look, Jaine. I thought it over and I'm prepared to hold the job open for the next few weeks, in case the police make an arrest and the case is cleared up."

At last, a ray of sunshine. Maybe life wasn't so bad after all.

I thanked him profusely and assured him that the whole matter would be cleared up in no time. I hung up, feeling a lot better. Certainly the cops would find the killer in a few weeks.

But just in case they didn't, I intended to do it myself.

Chapter 13

Yes, I'd made up my mind to find Marybeth's killer. I'd start my investigation right then and there. First thing I needed was a list of the club members' addresses and phone numbers. So I got on the phone and called Pam.

"Can you believe the nerve of the *Times* running our pictures like that?" she said when she heard my voice. "I may never work in showbiz again. Not that I'm working now. But it's the principle of the thing."

"At least they ran a nice photo of you."

"It's a publicity still from *Hedda Gabler*. I'm lucky they didn't run a shot of me as Felix Unger."

We both laughed hollow laughs.

"What are we going to do, Jaine? The publicity is just awful."

"Try not to worry. As soon as the police find the killer, we'll be off the hook."

"But what if they don't find the killer? What if it takes forever? These things can drag out for months, even years."

"Actually, that's why I'm calling."

I told her about my part-time career as a private eye, and how I was going to investigate the murder.

"Wow," she said, "I never would have figured you for a detective. You don't seem the type."

"I know I seem like a sniveling weakling—and I am—but

somehow, the endorphins kick in when I'm involved in an investigation."

"Really? I'm a congenital coward myself. But if there's anything I can do to help—"

"As a matter of fact, there is. Can you fax me the addresses and phone numbers of the club members?"

"Of course. Anything else you need?"

"Not right now. Not unless you happen to know who did it."

"Nope," she sighed. "If you ask me, the only person capable of murder in the PMS Club was Marybeth."

I had to agree with her on that one.

"Good luck, Jaine," she said. "I'll keep my fingers crossed. Call me if you need me for a stakeout or something. That might be fun."

I assured her I'd give her a ring if I needed company on a stakeout, and a few minutes later, she faxed me the addresses.

Then, after a quick shower, I got dressed and headed out the door to go killer hunting.

I was halfway down the path to my Corolla when I heard Lance calling me. He came running out of his apartment in shorts and a T-shirt, not an ounce of fat visible anywhere except in the cream cheese he was scarfing down on a toasted bagel. Tucked under his arm was a copy of the *Times*.

"You poor thing. I saw the story in the paper." He shook his head in sympathy. "Passport photo?"

"Nope. Driver's license."

"You ought to demand a retraction."

"I don't think they can retract a photo, Lance."

"Too bad," he said, licking cream cheese off his thumb. "The cops don't really think you have anything to do with the murder, do they?"

"I hope not."

"Didn't you tell them about all the murders you've solved?"

"I mentioned it to the lieutenant in charge of the case, but he didn't seem very impressed."

Lance polished off the last of his bagel and put his arm around me.

"I'm sure everything will be okay, hon. Although I guess it's hard for you to cope, what with your PMS."

Didn't anyone actually read beyond the headlines anymore?

"I don't have PMS," I said, pulling away in annoyance. "It's just the name of the club. It's actually a support group."

"For someone who doesn't have PMS, you're awfully snippy. But I understand," he said, patting my arm. "You're under a lot of pressure. If you need anything, just let me know."

"Thanks, Lance."

"By the way, this may not be the best time to ask, but I don't suppose you could fix me up with Colin. He's awfully cute."

He gazed down at Colin's picture in the paper. Luckily for Colin, the *Times* had run a decent photo of him, one in which he actually resembled a member of the human race.

I blinked in disbelief.

"Lance, the guy is a suspect in a murder case. He could be a killer."

"I'll take my chances."

"You're nuts."

"C'mon. Just give him my number."

"Okay," I sighed. "But don't blame me if he stands you up. Or knocks you off."

I waved good-bye and got in my Corolla. I'd decided to start my investigation where the whole mess began. At Rochelle's. As unlikely as it seemed, maybe Rochelle was the killer. After all, she was the one who made the guacamole. And she was the one with the strongest motive. Hadn't she told Marybeth, in no uncertain terms, to drop dead? Maybe the shy little mouse had gone bonkers and poisoned the woman who'd stolen her man. It wouldn't have been the first time.

Yes, my first stop would be a chat with Rochelle Meyers. Actually, my second stop. My first stop would be Junior's Restaurant, for some bacon and eggs and an English muffin dripping with butter.

Several news vans were parked outside Rochelle's house when I got there. I drove past them onto Rochelle's driveway, scrunched down in my seat, hoping the reporters wouldn't recognize me.

No such luck.

"Look!" a beauty pageant winner in Armani shouted. "It's one of the suspects."

Damn. If I looked like my driver's license photo, I was in deep doo doo. Maybe I ought to start using the Age-Defying Miracle Moisturizer my mother had sent me from the shopping channel. (Only $27.99, plus shipping and handling.)

"It's the writer," I heard another one shout. "Whatshername. Charlotte Bronte."

I scurried out of the Corolla, ignoring their questions.

When I rang the bell, an angry male voice shouted: "Go away! We're not talking to reporters!"

I assumed it had to be Marty Meyers, Rochelle's lying cheating sonofabitch husband.

"I'm not a reporter; I'm a member of the PMS club. Jaine Austen."

"Let her in, Marty," I heard Rochelle say.

The lying cheating sonofabitch opened the door.

I have to admit, I was surprised. I'd expected a slick Beverly Hills dentist straight off the set of *Extreme Makeover,* with graying temples and tassels on his Gucci loafers. But Marty was a big soft teddy bear, with a fuzzy crew cut and generous love handles hanging over his Gap khakis. Instead of a suave lothario, he looked like a guy buying plumbing supplies at Home Depot.

And that wasn't the only surprise in store for me. I blinked, somewhat taken aback, to see his arm curled lovingly around Rochelle's shoulder. Another entry for Mr. Ripley: Rochelle was beaming up at him, like a teenager with her first crush. For someone who was the prime suspect in a murder case, she looked amazingly chipper.

"Jaine, come on in," she said, smiling warmly. "Can I get you something to eat? Marty and I just finished breakfast. I made blueberry crepes, and homemade sticky buns."

Huh? If The Blob had done to me what Marty had done to her, I'd be serving him Raid on toast.

"No, thanks," I stammered. "I just ate."

"Are you sure. The sticky buns are awfully good, aren't they, honey?"

Honey? She's calling him *honey?*

"They're terrific, Ro," Marty said, gazing down with unabashed love.

What the hell was going on here? They'd gone from a couple on the brink of divorce to The Cleavers in less than 48 hours.

Rochelle must have sensed my confusion because she said, "Oh, Jaine. Isn't it wonderful? Marty and I are back together again. Come into the den, and we'll tell you all about it."

So we trooped off to the den, a wood-paneled hideaway with a large-screen TV and leather furnishings picked out no doubt by the recently deceased Marybeth.

"We feel funny sitting in the living room," Rochelle said, "after what happened there. I'm definitely going to have to change the furniture. But one thing's for sure: This time, I won't be using a decorator."

Rochelle and Marty sat down next to each other on a burgundy leather sofa. I sat across from them in a matching wing chair. Marty put his arm around her, and she snuggled close to him. He stroked her shoulder. She put her hand on his knee. If this kept up, any minute now they'd be necking.

I could contain myself no longer.

"If you don't mind my asking—what happened?"

"Marty wasn't going to leave me," Rochelle said. "Marybeth was lying."

"I was crazy to get involved with Marybeth," Marty said, shaking his head. "I don't know what came over me. Male midlife crisis, I guess." He shrugged sheepishly. "After a few months, I realized I'd made a mistake, and how much I still loved Rochelle. She's a finer woman than Marybeth could have ever dreamed of being. I told Marybeth it was all over between us. But she wouldn't listen. That's when she put that picture in my dresser drawer."

"She must've slipped it in while she was working on the bathroom," Rochelle said. "She wanted me to find it. She wanted to break up the marriage."

"Oh, God, Rochelle." Marty put his head in his hands. "I was so awful to you. I hate myself for that."

And then suddenly, he was crying. This big lug of a guy was sobbing his eyes out. Rochelle handed him a lace hanky from her pocket. It looked like a postage stamp in his big hands. He blew his nose with a mighty blast.

"Can you ever forgive me?" he sobbed.

"Of course I can," Rochelle said, stroking his crew cut.

I don't know if I'd have been so quick to forgive a man who cheated on me with my decorator, but clearly Rochelle was a more noble soul than I. And I have to admit that, in spite of my determination to hate the guy, I found myself touched by his tears.

"This is so embarrassing," he said, giving Rochelle's hanky a final blast.

"Not at all," I said. "It's good to see a man in touch with his emotions."

"I'd better get going," he said. "I hate leaving you alone with those vultures outside, Rochelle, but Mr. Nevin's molar is abscessed and he's in a lot of pain."

"That's okay," Rochelle assured him. "I'll be fine."

"I won't be long," he said.

Then he bent down and kissed her on the forehead.

"Very nice meeting you," he said to me, smiling sheepishly. "Forgive the dramatics."

"Nothing to forgive."

He clomped out the door, and when he was gone, Rochelle turned to me.

"Are you sure you don't want a sticky bun? They're nice and gooey."

"No, I couldn't. Really."

But you know me. Two minutes later, I was sitting in Rochelle's sunny yellow and blue French provincial kitchen, sipping fresh-brewed coffee and scarfing down a warm sticky bun studded with cinnamon and topped with a thick layer of creamy icing. I'd died and gone to Pastry Heaven.

"It's ironic," Rochelle said, as she watched me inhale my bun. "Now that our marriage is back on track, I'll probably be carted off to jail." For the first time since I walked in the front door, she looked worried. "I know the cops think I did it. The only fingerprints on the bottle of peanut oil were mine."

"That doesn't mean anything. Whoever doctored the guacamole probably held the bottle with a dishtowel, or an oven mitt."

"I know, but the police still think I did it." She shook her head and sighed. "Lieutenant Clemmons advised me to get an attorney. Marty's already lined up someone. He says he's the best around."

I sure hoped he was. Something told me she'd be needing a very good attorney, indeed.

"You've got to believe me, Jaine," she said, "I didn't kill Marybeth. I could never do a thing like that."

"I believe you." And I did. There was no doubt in my mind. Rochelle simply didn't have it in her to be a killer. It's funny. I'd started the case to get that job at Union National. But now, sitting here with Rochelle, I felt a sudden urge to protect her.

"Actually," I said, licking the last of the icing from my fingers, "that's why I'm here. I'm investigating the murder."

"I don't understand. I thought you were a writer."

"Yes, but I do some investigating on the side."

"That's so wonderful," she sighed, brushing a stray wisp of hair back into her ponytail. "Everybody has such exciting careers, and I just sit around baking things."

"You've got to stop putting yourself down, Rochelle. You're an extremely talented woman. I could never do half of what you do."

"That's awfully nice of you to say," she said, blushing with pleasure.

"I mean it."

Clearly unused to compliments, she jumped up from her chair and headed for the coffeepot. "Let me get you some more coffee. And help yourself to another bun."

"No, no. I couldn't possibly."

Okay, so I could. And I did. And it was delicious.

"Anyhow," I said, "I figure that as long as Marybeth's killer is at large, we're all under a cloud of suspicion. So I've decided to give the police a helping hand, whether they want one or not."

"That's the truly terrible thing about all this," Rochelle said. "The thought that one of my friends could be a killer."

"Did you notice any of the club members going into the kitchen alone on the night of the murder, anyone who could have doctored the guacamole?"

"No. But you saw what I was like that night. By the time you showed up, I'd had a margarita or three. I was blotto.

"It had been a terrible day. First the plumbers came to install some last-minute fixtures and they wound up breaking a pipe, which took them hours to fix. And then later in the afternoon the building inspector showed up and said he couldn't give us a permit—something about a missing gasket. And then, of course, I found that horrible picture of Marybeth."

She shuddered at the memory.

"That's when I started sucking up the margaritas. By the time you guys showed up, I was really out of it."

"What about Colin? He was here before anybody else. Could he have possibly sneaked into the kitchen while you weren't there?"

She took a thoughtful sip of her coffee. "It's hard to remember. I thought he went straight upstairs to the bathroom, and didn't come down again till after you and Pam had shown up. But I could be wrong. I was in such a daze. An elephant could've been doing a polka on my microwave and I wouldn't have noticed."

So it *was* possible. Colin could have tiptoed down the steps and added some peanut oil to the guacamole.

Of course, there was one other man I had to ask about: the teddy bear.

"Look," I said, "this is incredibly awkward, but what about Marty?"

Her eyes widened, shocked.

"What do you mean?"

"His affair with Marybeth had gone sour. He wanted to break things off. And she was giving him a hard time. Are you sure he didn't sneak home some time after four and touch up the guacamole?"

"No," she said, shaking her head, "he couldn't have possibly done it. He was down in Laguna."

"What was he doing in Laguna?"

"There's an art gallery there that we like. He went there to buy some paintings for his office. In fact, right after I found the picture of Marybeth, I called his office. I wanted to have it out with him, but his receptionist told me he was in Laguna. I thought she was lying, that he was with Marybeth. But he really was down in Laguna. Yesterday, I called the gallery and checked. And so did the police. Marty's in the clear."

Frankly, I was relieved Marty had an alibi. In spite of the fact that he'd behaved abominably toward Rochelle, he didn't seem like an evil man. Picturing him as a killer was like trying to picture Smoky the Bear with an Uzi.

But Colin Lambert, the resentful assistant—him, I wasn't so sure about.

Chapter 14

I showed up at Colin's apartment unannounced. He came to the door in a T-shirt and cutoffs—yet another guy with thighs thinner than mine.

"Jaine," he said, puzzled at the sight of me. "What're you doing here?"

"Actually—"

"Don't tell me. You came because you wanted a shoulder to cry on. I saw that picture in the paper. You ought to sue."

"Well, no. That's not why I'm here. I'm investigating Marybeth's murder."

"Oh?"

Was it my imagination, or was there suddenly a guarded look in his eyes?

"I work part-time as a private investigator," I explained.

"Really?" he said, ushering me inside. "How very *Charlie's Angels.*"

I took one look at his living room and stifled a gasp. How can I best describe it? What's the one word that sums it all up? Or, as the French would say, *le mot juste?*

After careful thought and many trips to the thesaurus, here's what I've come up with: *Acccck!*

Colin's living room was a blinding combination of lime green walls, potted palms, zebra-skin rugs, and sequined throw pillows. Tarzan meets Elton John.

"Striking, isn't it?" he asked.

Yeah. Like a migraine.

"Say hi to Max."

He walked over to one of the potted palms, where I saw a bright yellow parrot perched in the branches. Colin held out his finger, and Max jumped on board.

"Max, honey," Colin cooed to the bird, "say hi to Jaine. Say *Hi, Jaine.*"

The parrot looked at me with weary eyes and pooped onto the zebra skin rug.

"Dammit, Max. How many times have I told you? Poop in your cage, not on the rug."

He put the bird inside an ornate wrought-iron birdcage, the bottom of which was lined with old publicity stills of Marybeth.

"Go ahead. Make doo doo on the nice lady," he instructed the bird.

"I know it's awful," he said, turning to me, "having Max defecate on the dead. I'm disgraceful, aren't I?"

And then he shot me a smile that undoubtedly melted many a heart in West Hollywood.

"So, Jaine," he said. "How can I help you?"

"Mind if I ask you some questions?"

"Not at all. Have a seat."

He gestured to a hot pink velvet sofa that looked like it had spent its formative years in a New Orleans bordello.

"I'd offer you something to eat, but all I've got is some take-out soy sauce. I'm not much of a cook. But I make a mean cup of French-roast coffee. Want some?"

I'd just had three cups at Rochelle's, plus one at Junior's, and a cup of instant at home. If I had any more coffee I'd be bouncing off the potted palms. On the other hand, if he left the room, I'd have a chance to snoop around.

"Sure," I said, "coffee sounds great."

"I won't be long," he said, as he headed off to the kitchen.

"Take your time," I called out after him.

The minute he was gone I made a beeline for an old rolltop desk in the corner. The desk was littered with unpaid bills and sketches of wildly colored rooms. I could see why Marybeth had been reluctant to make Colin a partner. I didn't think there were many clients (outside of a Hollywood Boulevard massage parlor) who wanted their rooms done up in black leather and red lace.

I quickly rifled through the drawers but found little of interest. Until I discovered a tiny drawer under the lip of the rolltop desk. A secret compartment if ever I saw one. I pulled it open, and as I did, a piercing alarm filled the room.

Damn. The drawer was wired! I looked down and saw nothing in it but some fabric swatches. Why the hell would Colin have an alarm on his swatches?

Colin came ambling out from the kitchen with two mugs of steaming coffee, not the least bit perturbed at the racket.

"Oh, Max," he said. "Shut up."

And then I realized it wasn't an alarm making all that noise; it was the bird.

"Sorry about that," Colin said. "Max has learned how to imitate the sound of the car alarms in the neighborhood. It drives me nuts."

"I was just admiring your designs," I said, nudging his drawer shut with my hip. "They're great."

"I know. Can you believe Marybeth wanted to hire that guy from New York over me?"

He joined me at the desk and handed me my coffee.

"I like this one a lot," he said, pointing to one of the designs.

"Yes," I gushed. "What a great kitchen."

"It's not a kitchen," he said, frowning. "It's a bathroom."

"Oh? Isn't that a microwave?"

"No, it's a medicine cabinet."

Oops. This wasn't going nearly as smoothly as I'd hoped.

"Well," I said, "if you don't mind answering some questions . . ."

I skittered back to the sofa and took a seat.

He sat down opposite me on a zebra-skin ottoman.

"Go right ahead. Ask away."

"Actually, Rochelle thinks the cops have her pegged as Marybeth's killer."

"Can't say I blame them. She was crazy that night."

"Just for the record, though, did you see anyone go into the kitchen who could've tampered with the guacamole?"

"Nope," he said. "Just Rochelle. But I wasn't paying much attention. I suppose somebody else could've slipped in."

"Do you know any of the club members who might have had a grudge against Marybeth?"

He shook his head.

"Nobody really liked her, but nobody hated her enough to kill her."

"I'm not so sure about that," I said.

"Why? What do you mean?"

This wasn't going to be easy, but I took a deep breath and plowed ahead.

"Look, Colin. I heard you on the phone the night Marybeth announced she was bringing in that guy from New York. If I remember correctly, you said *I'd like to kill that bitch*. The exact same thing you said to Pam and me the night of the murder."

Colin rolled his eyes.

"For crying out loud, if I had a dollar for every time I said I wanted to kill Marybeth, I could retire tomorrow. You're a writer. Haven't you ever heard of the expression 'figure of speech'?"

He got up and began pacing on his zebra skin rug.

"I admit I was furious when she announced she'd hired that guy from New York. For years, she'd been promising me that she'd make me a partner, while I slaved like a dog, picking up her dry cleaning and her frappuccinos. And then she turned around and screwed me. So, yes, I was pissed. But I didn't kill her."

And I have to admit that, standing there in his *Desperate Housewives* T-shirt, Colin sure didn't look much like a killer.

"You're talking to a man who once liberated the lobsters from a lobster tank in a Chinese restaurant. I'm just not the murdering kind."

Just as I was trying to picture Colin unleashing lobsters in a Chinese restaurant, his cell phone rang.

"Yes?" he said, snapping it on. "Yes, this is Colin Lambert. . . . She did? Really?" His eyes lit up. "This afternoon? Why, yes. Yes, of course, I can be there."

He hung up and whooped with joy. "Omigod. That was Marybeth's attorney. That dear woman has named me in her will! I'm going to the reading of the will this afternoon!

"Max, baby," he crooned to the parrot, "pack your bird-seed, you're gonna be movin' on up to that de-luxe birdcage in the sky!"

He plopped down next to me on the sofa and hugged a throw pillow to his chest. "Maybe all those years of schlepping frappuccinos weren't a total loss."

Then he saw the look on my face and stopped cold.

"Damn," he said, clearly reading my mind. "I guess this means I had a motive to kill her, huh?"

I nodded.

"But I had no idea she was leaving me anything. Honest. This was a woman who used to give me drugstore candy for Christmas. Who would've dreamed she'd remember me in her will?"

He looked at me imploringly. "I swear, I didn't know."

And I believed him. He'd seemed genuinely surprised at that phone call from Marybeth's lawyer.

I thanked him for his time and got up to go, beginning to think he might be innocent after all. But as I was heading to the door, I happened to look up at his bookshelf and saw something that put him right back on my suspect list. There, sitting squashed between an *Architectural Digest* and a Christopher Lowell decorating book, was a cookbook. And not just any cookbook.

The title of this slim volume was *Cooking with Peanuts.*

I figured I'd stop by Doris's place next, to question the PMS Club's senior member. But when I got into my Corolla and checked my answering machine, I found an urgent message from Nick Angelides, the president of Toiletmasters, asking me to write him a funny speech to give at the L.A. Plumbers Association that night.

As much as I wanted to continue my investigation, I had an impressive collection of bills to pay. So I went home and spent the rest of the afternoon writing toilet humor for Phil. (*And so, my friends, I'd like to conclude my speech with this thought: People who live in glass houses should use their neighbor's bathroom.*)

After faxing Phil the speech, and my bill, I ran out to McDonald's for a quick dinner of a Quarter Pounder with fries, which I ate parked at the curb in front of my duplex. I still felt funny about eating high-calorie food in front of Prozac, what with her being on such a strict diet.

I slurped down the last of my Coke and popped a Listerine Cool Mint breath strip in my mouth so Prozac wouldn't smell the burger on my breath.

"Hi, honey. I'm home," I said, as I walked in the door.

I picked her up from where she was stretched out on the sofa on one of my cashmere sweaters. She didn't seem to have lost any weight yet. But she'd only been on her diet a few days. I'd be noticing the difference soon enough.

"How's my little angel?"

She sniffed suspiciously.

Is that a Quarter Pounder I smell underneath the Cool Mint breath strip?

I swear, this cat was a CIA operative in a former life.

"Okay," I admitted. "I had a Quarter Pounder. But that's it. No fries. Honest."

She shot me a piercing look.

"Okay, so I had fries. I'm ashamed of myself. I have absolutely no will power whatsoever."

Scratch my back for the next three hours, and I may forgive you.

I spent the rest of the night watching TV in bed, Prozac draped over my tummy as I scratched her back. Finally, I called it a day and turned out the light. But sleep didn't come easy. My mind kept drifting back to Colin, wondering what a guy who didn't cook was doing with a peanut cookbook.

Planning a recipe for murder, perhaps?

Chapter 15

Prozac continued to amaze me. The next morning she polished off her plate of Fit 'N Trim Tuna Tidbits with nary a whimper. Any day now, I expected to wake up and find her doing aerobics.

"I'm so proud of you, pumpkin face," I said, kneeling down and scratching her behind her ears.

Please. Don't call me "pumpkin face." "Prozac" is bad enough.

She shot me a blast of tuna breath, then scooted off to her perch on the living room sofa.

I went to the refrigerator to see what I could rustle up for my breakfast, hoping against hope to find something edible. But all I saw was the same moldy Swiss cheese and martini olives that were there the last time I looked. I'd have to run out and get something.

I was just heading to the bedroom to get dressed when there was a knock on my front door.

It was Lance.

"I come bearing breakfast," he said, holding up a care package from Junior's deli. "Coffee and corn muffins. Slathered with butter."

Prozac, who'd been snoozing on the sofa, sat up with interest. Food has that effect on her.

She jumped down off the sofa and came trotting over, her nose twitching inquisitively.

Do I smell bacon?

"It's only corn muffins," I said. "You don't like corn muffins."

She didn't look convinced.

Maybe I do, and maybe I don't.

"Say, Lance, would you mind if we ate our breakfast in the bathroom?"

"Huh?"

"I know it sounds silly, but now that Prozac's on her diet, I feel guilty eating anything more than five calories in front of her. She has this way of staring at me like those big-eyed kids in the Save the Children commercials."

"You're crazy. You know that, don't you?"

"Just humor me, okay?"

With an exasperated sigh, he followed me into the bathroom, where we ate our muffins perched on the edge of my tub.

"See?" I said. "Eating here's not so bad."

"Yeah, it's real handy if you need to floss."

"Aren't you proud of me?" I smeared my corn muffin with a glob of strawberry jam. "Prozac's actually been eating her diet food. And you didn't think I could tough it out."

"If you're so tough, why are we eating on a bathtub?"

"A mere technicality. The fact is, in the battle of wills, I finally scored a victory over Prozac."

"Well, congratulations," Lance conceded, clunking my coffee container in a toast. "Here's to Jaine, the Conqueror. Although I must say, Prozac doesn't look any thinner."

"That's because she just started eating healthy. I'm sure we'll be able to see the difference any day now."

Lance took a sip of his coffee and got down to the real reason for his visit.

"So. Did you mention me to Colin?"

"Trust me. You don't want to meet him. He's got lime green walls, a parrot who thinks he's a car alarm, and possible homicidal tendencies."

"He also happens to have cheekbones to die for. I'll take my chances. Just set me up with him, all right?"

"I don't know, Lance. I feel funny about it."

He grabbed the bag of muffins.

"Fix me up, or you don't get any more muffins."

"For crying out loud, if you think I'd sacrifice your safety for a lousy corn muffin—"

"Slathered with butter and strawberry jam," he reminded me.

"Okay, okay," I said, snatching the bag from him. "I'll do it."

One and a half muffins later (okay, two muffins), I was walking Lance to the door when the phone rang.

It was, of all people, Colin.

"I went to the reading of Marybeth's will yesterday," he said. "Meet me for lunch and I'll tell you all about it."

I could hear Max in the background, doing his ear-splitting rendition of a car alarm.

"How about the Earth Café?" I suggested. "One o'clock?"

"Great. See you then."

"Was that Colin?" Lance asked when I hung up.

"How did you know?"

"I heard a parrot impersonating a car alarm in the background."

I wasn't surprised he'd heard Max. The man can hear hair dryers blowing in Pomona.

"Yes, that was Colin."

"So you'll tell him about me?"

I reluctantly agreed to play cupid, and Lance left to get ready for work.

I still couldn't believe he wanted to meet Colin. Lance is a guy who'll pore over 37 articles in *Consumer Reports* before buying a toaster, and here he was ready to leap headlong into a relationship with a potential murderer without a second thought.

First Daddy, now Lance. Men are impossible, *n'est-ce pas?*

But I didn't have time to ponder the nutty nature of the male Homo sapiens, not while there was a killer on the loose.

I put in a call to Doris, but she wasn't home. Ashley, however, picked up on the first ring. I explained that I was looking into Marybeth's death and asked if I could come over to talk to her.

"I was just about to leave for the Brentwood Day Spa," she said. "Why don't you meet me there? I'm having a full-body seaweed wrap. You can have one, too."

"A seaweed wrap?"

"It's marvelous, darling. Your pores won't know what hit them."

Now I was born in Hermosa Beach, so I know all about seaweed. It's brown stinky stuff. The last thing I wanted to do was wrap my body in it. But I had a murder to solve. And if I had to turn myself into a seaweed sandwich to do it, so be it.

An hour later I was lying naked on a massage table while a nymph named Aloe (I'm not kidding; I came *thisclose* to asking if her middle name was Vera) slathered my body with a vile-smelling brown gunk.

"I know it smells awful," said Ashley, who was being slathered on a table next to me, "but the stuff works miracles."

"Yes," Aloe enthused, "kelp is nature's antioxidant. It sucks all the impurities out of your pores, and it breaks down your cellulite, although with all your cellulite, I'm not sure kelp will be strong enough. We may need to use dynamite."

Okay, she didn't really make that crack about dynamiting my cellulite. But I saw the look in her eyes when she was putting the seaweed on my thighs. She was thinking it.

"Don't you feel marvelous?" Ashley sighed.

Yeah. Like a crab at high tide.

"Marvelous," I echoed feebly.

At first I'd felt embarrassed about getting naked in front of Ashley. But I was heartened to see that, out of her designer clothes, Ashley was packing a few extra pounds of her own, in the dreaded hip/thigh area. Nothing like somebody else's fat to improve your own body image.

Once we were covered head to toe in marine ooze, Aloe and her fellow masseuse left Ashley and me alone in our private massage room.

"We'll be back in a half-hour," Aloe chirped, "as soon as you've absorbed your kelp."

"I thought they'd never leave," Ashley said the minute they were gone. "Now tell me about your investigation. I think it's wonderful that you're trying to help Rochelle. And I'm so impressed that you're a private eye."

"Just part-time."

"It sounds so exciting. Except for the footwear." Her brow furrowed, turning the seaweed on her forehead into tiny rivulets of mud. "I suppose you have to wear sensible shoes on the job?"

"Usually, yes."

"Too bad. There's always something, isn't there?"

I liked Ashley, but I was beginning to think she was just a tad shallow.

"So how can I help you?" she asked. "What did you want to know?"

"For starters, did you see anyone go into the kitchen alone the night of the murder?"

"No." Her blue eyes gazed out mournfully from behind the gunk on her face. "I'm afraid the only one I saw was Rochelle."

"What about Colin? He showed up at the house before any of us. Do you think he might have done it?"

She waited a beat before answering.

"I didn't want to say anything to the police, but to tell you the truth, if I had to guess one of us, I'd pick him. He was furious when he found out Marybeth had passed him over for partner. And he does have a temper. I remember Marybeth telling me that he once got so frustrated over a job they were working on, he punched a hole through the wall with his fist."

Very interesting, I thought, filing that tidbit away for future reference.

After a half-hour of marinating in seaweed, Ashley and I were hosed down and then polished off with a final coat of body lotion.

"Made from genuine algae," Aloe informed me, proudly holding out the jar.

Great. I always wanted to smell like the bottom of a fish tank.

But actually, it didn't smell too bad. Just a faint musky odor. And I have to confess that when Ashley and I headed off to the locker room to get dressed, I felt marvelous. Relaxed and invigorated at the same time. Maybe there was something to this seaweed therapy after all.

"What I don't understand," Ashley said, slipping into a pair of pink velour sweats that cost more than my wedding dress, "is why anyone would want to kill Marybeth. Sure, she got on everyone's nerves, but underneath it all, she was a wonderful person."

"Really?"

Somehow I had a hard time believing that.

Ashley smiled wryly.

"Okay, maybe she wasn't so wonderful. Not at the end. But I remember when I first met her, back in college. She was a lot different then. Very sweet and unaffected. That Little

Miss Sunshine act of hers that drove everybody crazy? Back then, it wasn't an act. She was a genuinely sunny, happy person."

She smiled at the memory.

"As the years went on, she got to be a pain in the ass, but I never stopped loving her."

Quickly, she reached for her imported British hairbrush and started blow-drying her hair. But not before I saw the tears well up in her eyes.

Well, alert the media. Somebody out there actually cared about Marybeth.

Or at least wanted me to think that she did.

Ashley hugged me good-bye in the parking lot of the Brentwood Day Spa, enveloping me in a cloud of massive boobs and designer perfume.

"Good luck, hon," she said. "I hope you catch Marybeth's killer. I'm just praying it turns out to be a dreadful accident, that whoever did it thought they were adding lime juice or something. Not very likely, though, is it?"

I shook my head no.

"Pity," she sighed. Then she got in her Jaguar and sped off, undoubtedly to work on her Black Belt in shopping.

As long as I was in Brentwood, I figured I'd swing by Doris's place. I'd checked out her address and saw that she lived not far from the spa, off San Vicente Boulevard, on Darlington Avenue.

Darlington was a leafy street lined with condos and townhouses. Parking was tight, but I managed to squeeze the Corolla between two SUVs and walked the half-block to Doris's New Englandy clapboard townhouse. I climbed the steps to her tiny front deck, lined with pots of hot pink impatiens, and rang the bell.

She came to the door in jeans and a denim work shirt. Her steel gray hair glinted in the morning sun.

"Jaine!" she said, flustered. "What are you doing here?"

"Actually, I wanted to talk to you about Marybeth's murder."

"Oh?" She stood there, making absolutely no move to invite me inside.

"Do you mind if I come in?"

I could practically see the wheels turning in her brain as she tried to think up an excuse to turn me away.

"It won't take long," I promised.

Reluctantly, she stepped aside.

"Why don't we go into the kitchen?" she said, taking me by the elbow and steering me straight toward the back of the townhouse. "I'll warm up some coffee."

Aloe had warned me not to drink coffee or alcohol for at least 24 hours, while I cleansed my system with herbal tea, preferably made from lemongrass, tree bark, or sassafras root.

Yeah, right. One of my major principles in life is to never drink shrubbery.

"Sure," I said. "Coffee sounds great."

Doris plunked me down in her tiny white-tile-and-pine kitchen, while she bustled around, fussing with a Mr. Coffee machine.

"Pam told me you were investigating the case," she said. "But it's so hard to picture you as a hard-boiled private eye."

"Everyone says that. I guess I'm more the soft-boiled type."

She shot me a blank stare. There was absolutely no sign of the hip, wisecracking Doris I'd met at the PMS Club. This woman getting mugs from her cupboard was a Stepford Doris.

"So what did you want to know?" she asked.

"Can you think of anyone other than Rochelle who might have had a motive to kill Marybeth?"

"No, not really. Except maybe Colin. I mean, she did pass him over for that job, didn't she?"

She handed me my coffee and faked a stiff smile.

"Really, Jaine, I already told the police everything I know, which isn't much."

"If you don't mind," I said, tossing a fake smile right back at her, "I'd really appreciate your going over it with me."

She sat down opposite me and began stirring her coffee.

"Did you see anyone go into the kitchen alone that night?" I asked. "Anyone who could've doctored the peanut oil?"

She didn't answer at first, just kept staring down into her mug and stirring her coffee so hard I thought she'd scrape the enamel off the mug.

Finally, she looked up.

"I didn't say anything about this to the police, because my memory's not what it used to be, but at one point while you and Pam and Ashley were upstairs, I left Rochelle and Colin in the kitchen and went to the living room to lay out cocktail napkins. After a while, I remember Rochelle coming into the living room to spike her margarita at the wet bar."

It didn't take a rocket scientist to figure out what she was trying to tell me.

"Which means Colin was alone in the kitchen?"

"If I'm remembering correctly. But I'm not really sure. Nowadays, my life is one big senior moment. That's why I didn't say anything to the police. What if I'm wrong?"

It was amazing how different Doris was here in her kitchen. At Rochelle's, she'd radiated confidence. Here, in the bright morning light, she was a befuddled woman who looked every one of her sixty-odd years.

We sipped our coffees, making idle chat about the murder.

"It's still so hard to believe that Marybeth is dead," she said. "All that energy, all that irritating positive thinking. She seemed so . . . indestructible.

"By the way," she added, "my condolences to you."

"To me? I hardly knew her."

"Not about Marybeth. About that picture of you they ran in the paper. You'll have a hard time living that one down."

She shot me a smile. So Wisecracking Doris wasn't dead, after all.

By now we'd finished our coffee, so I thanked her for her time, and she led me back to the front door. As we passed her living room, I couldn't resist peeking in. It was strange how she'd whisked me straight to the kitchen when I first showed up. I wondered if her place was a pigsty. Or maybe she had a stash of porn videos on her coffee table.

But no, it was a tasteful if somewhat bland living room. Standard sofa, arm chairs, fireplace. And a grand piano in the corner. But then I saw something that caught my attention. There, over the fireplace, was a portrait—of Doris and a man sitting together holding hands. Clearly they were a couple. A couple in love.

I stopped in my tracks.

"That's you, isn't it?" I asked.

She nodded, blushing.

I walked up to the portrait and saw that Doris and her companion were both wearing wedding bands. It had to be her husband. But hadn't Doris said she'd been through an ugly divorce? Not many divorced women I knew had pictures of their exes displayed over their fireplaces. On dartboards, maybe. But not over fireplaces.

"Is that your husband?"

"Yes," she sighed. "That's me and Glen. I was hoping you wouldn't see it."

I crossed over to the piano and saw dozens more pictures of Doris and her husband. Wedding photos. Holiday photos. Vacation photos. There was no mistaking the love in their eyes.

I shook my head, puzzled.

"I don't understand. I thought you hated the guy."

"I didn't hate him. On the contrary, I was very much in

love with him. He died nearly a year ago. It's much too pain-ful to talk about." Her eyes misted over with tears. "So I lie and tell people I'm divorced. It's easier that way."

She picked up one of the photos from the piano. It was a small photo, one I hadn't noticed, and handed it to me. In it, Doris sat by her husband's side, but now her husband was in a wheelchair, looking pale and gaunt.

"Two years ago, Glen was in a terrible car crash. It crip-pled him and caused internal injuries that eventually killed him. It was a slow, lingering death. I wouldn't wish it on my worst enemy."

By now the tears were streaming down her cheeks.

"See?" she said, wiping them away with the back of her hand. "Now you know why I can't talk about it."

So that's why she'd been acting so strange, why she'd been so flustered to see me. She didn't want me to discover the truth about her husband.

I felt like such a jerk, making her cry like that.

"I'm so sorry. I didn't mean to upset you."

"I'll live," she said, with a wry smile.

We said our good-byes and I headed out to my Corolla.

It's funny how you never know what's going on in people's lives. I'd never have guessed Doris was living with such a painful secret.

In the meanwhile, though, she'd tossed a very important piece of information in my lap—the juicy tidbit about Colin being alone in the kitchen the night of the murder. That, to-gether with the *Cooking with Peanuts* book I'd seen in his apartment, catapulted him to front runner in my Suspects Sweepstakes.

As I headed over to the Earth Café to meet him, I couldn't help feeling a bit apprehensive.

For all I knew, I had a lunch date with a killer.

Chapter 16

The Earth Café is a reasonably priced health food bistro in Beverly Hills, popular for their low-cal salads and wrap sandwiches. The kind of place skinny people go to load up on bean sprouts.

Huh? you're probably saying. *What's Jaine Austen, a gal who pops Quarter Pounders like Altoids, doing at a health food restaurant?*

Well, you've got a point. Normally health food and I go together like pizza and grits. But I'd decided to follow Prozac's shining example and watch my calories. If Prozac could summon up enough willpower to stick to her diet, there was no reason why I couldn't, right? After all, I was at least one hundred points ahead of her on the IQ scale. Well, twenty-five, anyway.

Colin was waiting for me at a wrought-iron bistro table in the café's charming outdoor patio. He wore chinos and a button-down baby blue oxford shirt, his dark blond hair cut short and spiky.

Could someone this cute and clean-cut really be a killer? Of course, he could. I wouldn't be surprised if 9 out of 10 crazed killers looked like models in a Gap commercial.

After exchanging greetings, we went inside and gave our orders to the guy behind the counter. You'll be proud to know I did not order a burger or fettucini alfredo. (Mainly because they didn't have burgers or fettucini alfredo on the menu.) Instead, I ordered a free-range turkey wrap, hold the mayo.

Colin got the jumbo roast beef wrap, extra mayo, with a side of potato salad. Life sure isn't fair, is it? The guy had a waist the size of my ankle and he was ordering extra mayo and potato salad.

Our sandwiches each came with a package of all-natural yam potato chips. Once again, you'll be proud to know I gave mine to Colin. After all, 120 calories was still 120 calories, natural or not.

"So how'd things go at the reading of the will?" I asked, as we dug into our food.

"What a bust," Colin said. "Marybeth's estate was worth nearly two million dollars and all she left me was a crummy armoire."

"How do you know it isn't valuable?"

"I was with her when she bought it. It cost her fifty bucks at an auction."

"That's too bad," I said.

"But," he noted, "at least it means I didn't have a motive to kill her."

I wasn't so sure about that. He could've tossed the peanut oil in the guacamole in a moment of rage, as payback for years of workplace abuse.

"So who got her money?" I asked.

"She left most of it to her relatives. There was a small bequest to her maid, and Ashley got ten grand. The one person who didn't need any money got ten grand. Talk about the rich getting richer."

He shook his head, disgusted.

"She could've at least left me her Porsche," he pouted, "considering all the times I took it to the car wash for her. Or a percentage of that lottery money she won. After all, I was the one who had to race out in rush-hour traffic to pick up the damn ticket for her, along with her daily frappuccino and chocolate chip muffin."

He took a desultory bite of his yam chip.

"I still can't believe she won that money. Some people have all the luck."

"Colin, she's dead. I think it's safe to assume she didn't have *all* the luck."

Colin had been so busy bitching about his inheritance he'd barely touched his sandwich. I, on the other hand, had wolfed mine down in record time. I thought about asking for my yam chips back, but I reined myself in. Really, I told myself, I'd had plenty to eat. More than enough. Me and my hips did not need any yam chips. End of story.

Besides, I had to stop thinking about food and get back on track with my questioning. It wasn't going to be easy, but I needed to confront Colin.

I took a deep breath and plowed ahead.

"Colin, I was just talking to Doris—"

"Oh?" A glob of mayonnaise oozed out from his wrap. Oh, Lord. Isn't mayonnaise heavenly? I wondered if he'd notice if I reached out and scooped it up with my finger. Of course, he'd notice! Was I nuts? I had to stop this nonsense and concentrate on the murder.

"Anyhow," I said, forcing myself not to stare at the mayonnaise, "Doris said she was certain she saw you alone in Rochelle's kitchen on the night of the murder."

Of course, Doris had said no such thing. She hadn't been certain at all, but I wasn't about to tell him that.

Colin's face clouded over.

"So? What if I was? I didn't go anywhere near that guacamole."

Bingo. My gambit had paid off. He *had* been alone in the kitchen. I tried to look as stern as possible.

"Colin, I saw the cookbook in your apartment."

"What cookbook?" He looked genuinely puzzled. "I don't cook."

"*Cooking with Peanuts.*"

He laughed.

"Oh, that. It was a gag gift, from my ex-boyfriend. He knew how much Marybeth got on my nerves and he gave it to me as a joke. Honest. Did you think I was sitting around dreaming up poisoned peanut dishes for Marybeth?"

He laughed again, as innocent as a choirboy.

It was then that I heard someone call my name.

"Jaine! Jaine Austen!"

I looked up and saw Lance coming our way, dolled out in his finest three-piece Armani.

"What a surprise running into you like this," he said, doing the worst acting job since *Attack of the Killer Tomatoes.*

He'd obviously overheard me making plans this morning and decided to take my matchmaking duties into his own hands.

"Aren't you going to introduce us?" he said, ignoring me and grinning at Colin.

"Of course," I muttered. "Lance, Colin. Colin, Lance."

They locked eyeballs, and I could've been a bean sprout in my turkey wrap for all they cared.

The next thing I knew Lance had drawn up a chair at our table and he and Colin were talking about an upcoming revival of *Gypsy*.

I made a few feeble attempts to join in the conversation, but I'd morphed into the Invisible Woman. Any more chatter about the murder, I could see, was out of the question.

I mumbled an excuse about an urgent appointment, took back my yam chips, and ran.

I ate my chips in the Corolla while I checked my phone messages. Nick from Toiletmasters had called to tell me my speech "bowled them over," and Kandi called to tell me that the bridesmaid dresses had come in. She gave me the address of a bridal salon in Beverly Hills and told me to hurry over as soon as possible for my fitting. The last thing I wanted to do was squeeze myself into that ghastly frill festival Kandi had shown me. But sooner or later, I'd have to do it. And as long as I was already in Beverly Hills, I might as well get it over with.

So, after licking the last of the all-natural yam chip grease from my fingers, I put the Corolla in gear and headed off to the Amy Lee Bridal Salon.

Amy Lee was a stunning fortysomething Asian woman. In marked contrast to the gossamer bridal dresses that surrounded her, she wore a simple but impeccably tailored suit. Her glossy black hair was cut in a chin-length bob, with a bold streak of gray in front.

I told her I was there for Kandi's wedding. She looked me up and down appraisingly.

"Ms. Tobolowsky said you might present a challenge. And I can see she wasn't exaggerating. I'm going to have to jam you into that dress with a crowbar."

Okay, so she didn't really make the crack about the crowbar. She just nodded and got the dress.

I was hoping it wouldn't look quite as bad as it had in the ad Kandi had shown me. I hoped in vain. In person, the puffy sleeves were even puffier, the nipped-in waist was tourniquet tight, and the hips flared out like wings on a jumbo jet.

Somehow Amy managed to zip me into it.

I'd been afraid that I'd wind up looking like Cinderella on steroids. I was wrong. I looked like Cinderella's ugly stepsister on steroids.

Amy didn't even try to soothe me with lies.

"This happens all the time," she said. "The bride is so in love with the dress she doesn't realize it may not be flattering for her bridesmaids."

Amy summoned a seamstress from the back of the store, an elderly Asian woman who let out a steady stream of "tsk-tsks" as she pinned the dress for alterations.

At last, the torture was over, and I got back into my own clothes.

"How much do I owe you?" I asked Amy. I shuddered to think I was actually going to have to pay to look this awful.

"Ms. Tobolowsky is taking care of it."

"Oh, I couldn't possibly let her do that. It's out of the question. How much do I owe you?" I repeated, whipping out my credit card.

"Seven hundred dollars."

Seven hundred dollars??? On second thought, maybe I could let Kandi do it. After all, she had the money, and I didn't. Besides, even if I wanted to, I don't think my good pals at MasterCard would let the sale go through. I was perilously close to my credit limit as it was. A $700 charge would put me over the top, by about $699.

So I just smiled weakly and put my credit card away.

"I thought you might do that," Amy said, with a knowing smile. "Your dress will be ready tomorrow."

"Goody. I can't wait."

"Ms. Austen, let me tell you what I tell my other customers. I know you're unhappy with the dress, but just think how lovely the bride will look in comparison to you. Look at it this way. Wearing this dress will be your gift to her."

"Frankly," I said, "I'd rather give stemware."

I got home and plopped down on the sofa next to Prozac, who was hard at work licking her privates.

"Oh, Pro," I moaned. "There ought to be a law against puffy sleeves."

Prozac looked up from her genitals and sniffed.

Do I smell potato chips on your breath?

"Yes," I said, with as much dignity as I could muster, "but

they happen to be all-natural yam chips. Hardly any calories."

Hah.

Was it my imagination, or was she actually smirking?

"Just because you've stuck to your diet for a few days doesn't make you wondercat. Big deal. I've stuck to diets for weeks at a time."

She looked up from her genitals and shot me a look.

"Okay, days at a time."

She kept on staring.

"Okay, minutes at a time."

By now her eyes were practically boring a hole in my forehead.

"Okay, so I'm an abject failure at dieting. Just quit staring at me like that, willya?"

With what I could swear was another smirk, she went back to licking her privates.

One of these days I'm going to get myself a big, slobbering, uncritical dog.

In the meanwhile, though, I had bigger fish to fry.

I closed my eyes to concentrate on Marybeth's murder, but suddenly all I could picture was fish frying. Yes, wouldn't a nice big plate of fried shrimp be great right now? I could run out and get a Hungry Man Fried Shrimp TV Dinner. With French fries and extra tartar sauce. Yum.

What was wrong with me? I had to focus. I forced myself to go over the case. I'd interviewed all the club members and had pretty much gotten nowhere. The only thing I learned was that Colin was alone in the kitchen and owned a peanut cookbook. Not exactly evidence that would hold up in court.

I sure hoped the cops were making better progress than I was.

I needed to put on my thinking cap and see if I could come up with any other theories. So I did what I always do when I need to operate at top mental capacity. I made myself a strong cup of coffee, took out a legal pad, sharpened a batch of pencils—and spent the rest of the afternoon watching daytime TV.

What can I say? I needed the distraction. You know how it is. Sometimes when you're driving yourself crazy trying to solve a problem, the answer comes to you when you walk away from it.

I was in the middle of watching a highly educational program on Pregnant Women Who Cheat on Their Married Lovers when the phone rang.

"Hey, Nancy Drew." It was Pam. "How's it going with The Case of the Dreadful Decorator?"

I told her what little I'd learned so far, including Colin admitting that he was alone in the kitchen on the night of the murder.

"Do you think Colin's the killer?" she asked.

"So far, he's my most promising suspect. What do you think?"

"I hate to say it, because I really like the guy. But I've always thought Colin had a—how can I put it?—a moral weak spot. Like this one time we ate lunch together, and when we were through, I saw him steal the waiter's tip."

"You're kidding."

"No. Really. I never forgot it."

Yet another vote for Colin for killer.

"Too bad Marybeth didn't leave him big bucks in her will," I sighed. "It would've given him a much stronger motive to kill her."

"Yeah. Getting turned down for a job isn't exactly the most compelling motive in the world. If it was, I'd be on death row by now."

"All she left him was the armoire. He really wanted her Porsche."

"At least she won't be driving it anymore," she said. "It's funny, if you'd asked me to guess how Marybeth was going to die, I would've given you odds it would've been in that car. Marybeth was an accident waiting to happen.

"Hey," she said, interrupting herself, "do you suppose Colin was lying? Maybe Marybeth left him money after all, and he just didn't tell you."

"It would be a pretty silly lie, wouldn't it? After all, I could easily find out the truth from Ashley or Marybeth's attorney."

"You're right, of course. That's why you're the detective and I'm not."

We spent a few more minutes gabbing, Pam filling me in on the details of an audition she'd gone on for a fast food commercial.

"They wanted somebody ordinary looking, thank heavens. Of course, in Hollywood, ordinary means really pretty instead of smashingly gorgeous, but I showed up anyway, and the casting director seemed to like me. So keep your fingers crossed. Toes, too."

After promising to cross all my digits, I hung up and checked my watch. Only five P.M., but I was starving. I'd have a nice early dinner. I once read that eating dinner early was a favorite dieting technique of the celebrities. *Never eat anything after six,* the article said, *and the pounds will practically fly off your body.*

Yes, I'd run over to the supermarket and get myself a healthy salad at the salad bar. Just some greens, maybe a little chicken, a dribble of dressing, and scads of veggies. What a great idea. I was feeling thinner already.

I grabbed my car keys and drove over to the market, where I headed straight for the salad bar. I did not stop off at the cookie aisle, or the bakery section. True, I came perilously close to paying a visit to my friends Ben & Jerry in the freezer case, but I was strong. I walked resolutely past all those temptations. And when I got to the salad bar, I stayed strong and loaded up on the low-cal stuff. You'll be happy to learn that I Just Said No to the croutons, gloppy ranch salad dressing and giant chunks of cheese that were calling my name.

When I'd stuffed more greens into my container than I'd eaten in the last five years, I trotted over to the checkout counter, feeling quite proud of myself. I thought back to my lunch with Sam and Andrew, and how unappetizing the idea of a salad had seemed to me then. Now it seemed like the only sensible thing to be eating.

Maybe I'd finally reached the stage in life where dieting would be doable. Indeed, I'd probably reached a certain level of maturity necessary to start a healthy eating regimen and stick with it.

I paid for my salad and headed out the door, barely glancing at the Reese's Pieces at the checkout counter.

It looked like Prozac wasn't the only one with willpower in our family.

Back home, I tossed some Healthy Halibut Guts into Prozac's dinner bowl. She proceeded to peck at it daintily, like a supermodel on a dinner date.

Instead of wolfing down my meal standing up over the kitchen counter as I usually do, I decided to eat my diet dinner in style, another diet tip I remembered reading. *Eat your food slowly at the dinner table with a beautiful place setting. You'll eat less and feel fuller.*

So, clearing away a pile of unpaid bills, I put a pretty rattan placemat on my dining table, poured myself a teensy glass of chardonnay, and laid out my salad on a festive Christmas dinner plate my mom had sent me from the shopping channel. (Service for four, only $69.95 plus shipping and handling.)

Then I put a Tony Bennett CD on my stereo and sat down to eat. Or, shall I say, dine.

I took my first bite, chewing slowly, savoring all the natural tastes of the vegetables. How wonderful it was, I told myself, to be eating food that wasn't drenched in ketchup and salt.

I savored each and every bite of that meal. Okay, I savored the first three bites. After that, I couldn't help myself. I was starving. I tore into those vegetables like Bugs Bunny in a carrot patch. Before I knew it, I'd eaten every last morsel of the salad and was scooping the dressing off the plate with my finger.

By now Prozac had finished most of her halibut and was back on the living room sofa, taking an after-dinner pass at her genitals.

I eyed her leftover halibut hungrily. Actually, it didn't look all that bad. Hadn't I always been curious about how cat food tasted?

Don't get upset. Of course, I didn't eat it. What sort of desperado do you think I am? I would never sink so low, for heaven's sake. Besides, Prozac was watching and I knew I'd never get away with it.

I walked over to where she was lying on the couch, looking perfectly content.

"How the hell do you do it, Pro? How do you stay on that godawful diet of yours?"

She looked up at me and yawned.

Nothing to it. For thinner hips, just zip your lips.

"You're really beginning to get on my nerves. You know that, don't you?"

I headed to the bedroom to distract myself with some television.

But wouldn't you know, everywhere I looked I saw food. Lucy was eating that big plate of spaghetti in the booth next to Bill Holden, Emeril was cooking scampi swimming in garlic butter, and every station seemed to be playing the same commercial for the all-you-can-eat chicken parmigiana dinner at the Olive Garden restaurant.

I couldn't take it any more. I grabbed a sweater and headed for the door.

"I'm going out for a walk," I announced to Prozac.

You can't fool me. You're going for ice cream.

"You are so wrong," I insisted.

And she was. I did not go out for ice cream. Absolutely not.

I went out for Reese's Pieces.

I was sitting in my car, digging into my Reese's Pieces, when my mind drifted back to my conversation with Pam.

I suddenly had the feeling that she'd said something important, that she'd given me a valuable clue. But for the life of me, I couldn't put my finger on it. Exactly what had she said? Just that Marybeth was a terrible driver and that Colin had stolen a tip at a restaurant.

Of course, by now you've probably already figured it out. But I didn't. Not right then, anyway.

I headed home and hurried to the bathroom to brush my teeth so Prozac wouldn't smell the chocolate on my breath.

And that's when it hit me, while I was brushing my teeth. Something that Pam said came bubbling up to my consciousness: *Marybeth was an accident waiting to happen.*

I raced to the phone with toothpaste still in my mouth.

"Pam," I said, when I got her on the line, "it's me, Jaine."

"Are you okay? You sound funny."

"It's just toothpaste in my mouth. Look, I need to ask you something. I know Marybeth was a terrible driver, but was she ever actually in an auto accident?"

"I don't know. I'm not sure."

"Try to remember."

"Well, now that you mention it, when I first joined the PMS Club, Ashley was driving Marybeth to all the meetings. Do you think it's possible she'd had her license revoked?"

"Yes," I said, "I think it's very possible."

I got off the phone and hurried to my computer, where I logged onto the *L.A. Times* archives. What did Doris say her husband's name was? Glen. That was it. Glen Jenkins.

I typed in his name. Seconds later, a story popped on the screen about a terrible car crash on the San Diego Freeway. Tied up traffic for three hours. Several people were injured, one of them seriously, a Mr. Glen Jenkins.

The driver of the vehicle that caused the accident: Marybeth Olson.

So. Marybeth was the one who'd put Glen Jenkins in a wheelchair.

I whistled softly. It looked like Doris had just taken the lead away from Colin in my Murder Suspect Sweepstakes.

Chapter 17

When Doris answered the door the next day, she knew the jig was up. She had the same look in her eyes The Blob had when I caught him watching football in my Victoria's Secret teddy. But unlike The Blob, Doris wasn't the least bit flustered.

"Hello, Jaine," she said, gazing at me with steady gray eyes.

I handed her the printout I'd made of the *Times* article.

"Want to tell me about it?"

"Sure." Cool as a cucumber. "Come on in."

This time she didn't try to hustle me to the kitchen. She led me straight to the living room. We sat opposite each other on matching chenille sofas, under the portrait of Doris and Glen holding hands in happier days.

"So you know the truth," she said. "Funny, it's actually a relief. It's been hell keeping it bottled up inside me for so long."

She put her feet up on the coffee table, and I was surprised to see that she was wearing pink bunny slippers. No-nonsense Doris in bunny slippers? I guess you never know what people are going to wear in the privacy of their own homes, a lesson I should've learned after that episode with The Blob and my teddy.

She glanced down at the *Times* article, and her eyes grew hard.

"That bitch walked away from the accident without a scratch. And poor Glen never walked again. We never heard a word from her. No apology. No flowers. Not even a crummy get well card. For two years, I watched my husband die, day by day, all because of Marybeth."

She picked up the printout and crumpled it into a tight ball.

"After Glen died, I hired a private eye to track her down. I joined her gym and ingratiated myself with her friends. Eventually they asked me to join the PMS Club. I wasn't planning to kill her. Not at first, anyway. In the beginning, I just wanted to see what kind of person could walk away from a tragedy like that without a second thought. I thought that maybe once I got to know her she wouldn't be so bad, that I'd discover something about her that would explain her actions."

She shook her head, waving away that notion.

"But I hated her from the minute I met her. She was everything I feared she'd be, and worse. And so I knew I had to kill her."

Omigosh. She was confessing. Right here and now. The case was over. All I had to do was get her to sign a confession, and I could start working at Union National with the adorable Andrew Ferguson!

"I was going to drain the brake fluid from Marybeth's Porsche. Have her die in an auto accident. It would be poetic justice."

She smiled grimly.

If I ever wrote a memoir, I knew what the title of this chapter would be: *The Killer Wore Bunny Slippers!*

"But each time I tried to do it," she said, "I lost my nerve. It's not easy draining brake fluid from a car without attracting attention."

"So then you decided to poison her with peanut oil?"

"No," she said. "Then I got lucky. Somebody else killed her for me." She gave her bunny slippers a happy wiggle. "All's well that ends well, eh?"

"So you didn't put the peanut oil in the guacamole?"

"Nope," she said, her eyes glinting steely gray. "Wasn't me."

With that, she picked up the crumpled *Times* story and tossed it into the fireplace.

So much for her confession. I thanked Doris for her time and left her alone with her memories of Glen.

As I walked out to my Corolla I couldn't help wondering: If Doris had lied so convincingly about being divorced, who's to say she wasn't lying about the murder?

Maybe she didn't change her mind about killing Marybeth.

Maybe all she changed was her murder weapon.

Now I had two suspects with motives, but not a shred of proof that either one of them doctored the guacamole. The only fingerprints on that damn bottle of peanut oil were Rochelle's.

Feeling frustrated by my lack of evidence, I decided to drive out to the beach to clear my head. It was an overcast day, cool and gray, the perfect day for walking and thinking, with no TV to distract me.

I drove out to Malibu and parked on the Coast Highway, then scrambled down a steep pebbled path onto the beach.

Hardly anyone was there. Just a few dog walkers and hardy joggers, tossing up clumps of wet sand as they ran. I took off my shoes and walked along the shoreline, sand squishing between my toes. The cool, damp air felt great on my face. True, my hair was frizzing like a Brillo pad, but I didn't care. It was worth it.

I walked along the shoreline, turning things over in my mind. And after forty-five minutes of deep thought, I reached an important insight:

Dog poop doesn't smell nearly as bad at the beach as it does in town.

What can I say? My mind wandered.

Annoyed at myself for having frittered away forty-five minutes, I headed back to the Corolla.

I started the car and was about to merge into traffic on the Coast Highway when suddenly I heard an earsplitting explosion. Now I've seen my fair share of action flicks, so I know a gunshot when I hear one. Someone was shooting at me!

With Herculean effort, I managed to keep my cool and steered the Corolla into the ongoing stream of cars on the highway.

Yeah, right. You know me better than that. I immediately flew into an advanced state of panic and barely missed ramming my Corolla into a Mercedes SUV. The charming trophy wife behind the wheel flashed me an impressive set of diamonds as she gave me the finger.

I gunned the accelerator, once again trying to merge into traffic, when another shot rang in the air. Why the hell wasn't anyone stopping to help me? I could only pray that one of those cowards whizzing by on the highway would call the police.

Suddenly the Corolla started bumping erratically. Damn. The shooter had blown out my tires. I wasn't going anywhere. I was stranded, alone on the shoulder of the road with a would-be assassin.

I crouched down in my seat and peeked out the windows, looking for the gunman. But all I saw were joggers on the beach. Then I checked out the rearview mirror and let out a terrified scream. Staring back at me was a wide-eyed derelict. Omigod, how did he get in my car? What did he want from me? Had Marybeth's killer paid him to kill and/or seriously maim me?

With my heart pounding, I sneaked another peek in the

mirror. Strange, the derelict looked somewhat like me. I looked again. Oh, good heavens, it *was* me. My hair had gone completely haywire in the fog, giving me that finger-in-the-light-socket mental patient look.

When my heart finally stopped racing, I took another look outside. Still no sign of any gun-toting bad guys. But I wasn't taking any chances. No way was I getting out of my car. I got out my cell phone and called 911.

Five minutes later, a squad car pulled up.

Two Malibu cops, tan enough to moonlight as lifeguards, got out of the car. One of them approached my window while the other started examining the tires.

"Someone tried to kill me!" I wailed to the cop at my window. "They shot out my tires."

"Nobody shot your tires," his partner said, kneeling over the front passenger tire.

"What?"

"Come here and see for yourself."

Somehow I managed to pry my knuckles from the steering wheel and walked over to the front of the car.

"Looks like you ran over a box of nails."

Indeed, my front tires were studded with dozens of industrial-strength nails.

"Gosh, it sounded just like gunshots," I said, making a mental note to never again jump to conclusions based on movie sound effects.

The cop who discovered the nails shook his head, disgusted.

"What sort of jerk throws nails on the highway?"

"Probably kids," his partner said. "Probably thought it was funny."

Maybe it was kids, I thought. But maybe not. Maybe it was someone who wanted to intimidate me, and get me to stop my investigation.

No, I'd bet my bottom Pop Tart that the person who'd tossed those nails in the path of my car was Marybeth's killer.

Luckily, I have an instruction booklet called *How to Change a Tire* in my glove compartment, one of the many useful gifts my mom has sent me from the shopping channel. Which made for very interesting reading while the Triple A guy actually did the job. (C'mon now. You didn't really think that I, Jaine Austen, a woman who has trouble changing an overhead light bulb, was going to change her own tire, did you?)

By the time the Triple A guy drove off, my heart rate had finally returned to normal, and my hands had stopped shaking enough so that I could drive.

Before starting the car, I took another look at myself in my rearview mirror. Yikes. My hair really was a disaster. I looked like a cross between Little Orphan Annie and Albert Einstein.

I reached into my bag for my hairbrush to tame down my mop. But the brush I pulled out wasn't mine. My brush is a $2.79 plastic SavOn special. This brush was one of those fancy British boar bristle models. And then I recognized it. It was Ashley's brush, the one she was using at the Brentwood Day Spa. I must've grabbed it by accident in the locker room.

As long as I was out in Malibu, I decided to stop by Ashley's place and return it. If indeed the murderer was trying to get me to stop my investigation, it wasn't going to work. I may be a sniveling weakling, but nobody can say I'm not a foolhardy sniveling weakling.

Yes, I'd go to Ashley's. It would be a perfect opportunity to ask her some more questions. Maybe this time she'd remember seeing something incriminating.

If not, maybe she'd treat me to an expensive lunch. I sure could use one.

* * *

I drove up the winding road to Ashley's house—correction, palace—in Malibu. It was a sprawling Mediterranean extravaganza, studded with elaborate arches and balconies, very Tuscany-by-the-sea.

I was puzzled by the landscaping, though. All the plants were overgrown, and the lawn looked like it hadn't been mowed in weeks. Maybe this was the latest thing in landscaping: the Vacant Lot Look. Or maybe Ashley was simply between gardeners.

I rang her doorbell, but no one came to the door. After a minute or so, I rang again. Still no answer. Which surprised me, because Ashley's Jag was parked right there in the driveway. She had to be home. I pressed the buzzer one more time.

"Who the hell is it?" she finally called out.

"It's Jaine. Jaine Austen."

I heard the sound of footsteps approaching. Ashley opened the door, in a flowing silk caftan, holding a glass of what smelled like gin.

"Jaine!" She looked at me in dismay. "What are you doing here?"

Not exactly the warm and fuzzy greeting I'd been hoping for.

I smiled weakly and fished her hairbrush from my purse.

"I took your brush by mistake the other day, and I happened to be in the neighborhood so I thought I'd return it."

"Thanks, hon," she said, snatching it from me. "You're a doll for bringing it by."

She made no move to invite me in.

First Doris, now Ashley. Clearly these two were not fans of unexpected guests.

"Actually, I wanted to ask you a few more questions about the murder."

"Oh." She took a slug of her gin, still blocking the doorway.

"Mind if I come in?"

"Well, okay," she sighed. She stepped aside with a forced smile and led me past a huge echoing foyer into her living room.

I expected to see a room ripped from the pages of *Architectural Digest*. Instead, it looked like something from *Better Homes & Hovels*. There were large faded spots on the walls where paintings had once hung. And indentations in the carpeting where furniture used to sit.

Just a few pieces of furniture remained: A sofa, some folding metal chairs, and a cheap television perched on a card table. Throwaway newspapers and mail-order catalogues were tossed carelessly around the room.

"Excuse the mess," Ashley said, with a wave of her caftanned sleeve. "Maid's day off."

It looked more like the maid's month off. The dust was thick as velvet on the few pieces of furniture that were still in the room.

"Can I get you something to drink?" she asked. "I'm having a teeny tiny martooni."

"No, thanks. I'm fine."

"Have a seat," she said, slumping down onto the sofa. I know the place is a fright." She took a slug of her 'martooni.' "Most of the furniture's out being reupholstered."

Yeah, right, I thought, glancing up at the faded spaces on the walls. Since when do paintings get reupholstered?

I guess she must've sensed my skepticism.

"Oh, what the hell. I'm not fooling you, am I?" She polished off her booze in a single gulp. "I'm broke, honey. Busted. I can barely scrape enough together to afford this rotgut gin."

"But I don't understand. The other day. At the spa. It must have cost a fortune—"

"Gift certificates. I've been saving them for a special occasion. And when you called and said you wanted to come to the house, it was the first thing I could think of to keep you from seeing all this."

"I'm sorry you had to use up those certificates on my account."

"Don't be. I had fun. Didn't you?"

"Of course I did."

And I meant it. I really did have fun. The gals in the PMS Club were some of the most fun murder suspects I'd ever met.

"Remember that day I ran into you at Goodwill?" she said. "I wasn't dropping anything off. I was shopping there. When I saw you coming, I dumped what I'd bought in the trash and pretended that I'd just made a donation."

"Really?" I said, trying my best not to look like someone who'd fished her dry cleaning out of one of the donation bins.

"Yep, Goodwill's my speed nowadays," she said, nodding wistfully. "I've come a long way from Ferragamo."

"But everybody thinks you're—"

"Loaded? No way. Don't have a pot to piss in. When my sonofabitch husband died, he left me up to my eyeballs in debt. Thank God we owned the house. Otherwise, I'd be living out of my Jaguar." She gestured around the room. "For the past two years, I've been cashing in on the proceeds from our paintings and our furniture."

Why not do what the rest of the world does, I wondered, and get a job?

"Have you tried looking for work?" I asked.

"Easier said than done. You try competing for work with kids fresh out of college. Besides, employers don't exactly come banging on your door when you've got a B.A. in art history. Sure, I'd like to work for the Getty, but so far, the only people who want me are the friendly folks at Taco Bell.

Sometimes I work nights in the boiler room of a telemarketing company. It's an absolute hellhole but it's one place I'm sure I won't run into anyone I know. Which reminds me, please don't tell anybody about this. The one thing I've got left is my pride."

She brought her glass to her lips and then realized it was empty.

"Sure you don't want one of these?"

I shook my head.

"I don't blame you. It's awful stuff. You know you're in trouble when your gin is imported from Guam."

She got on her knees and began fishing around under the sofa.

"Where are you, you little devil?" Finally, she found what she was looking for.

"Aha!" She pulled out a bottle of Brand X gin and filled her glass, licking a few drops that spilled onto her hand.

So much for pride.

"I won't tell anyone," I promised, "but I can't believe anybody would think less of you if they knew the truth."

"Probably not. But I think less of me."

She slugged down some gin and belched softly.

"Oops." She covered her mouth and giggled. "*Excusez-moi!*"

Somebody was well on her way to getting tanked.

"I know it's crazy to keep up the pretense," she said, "but I can't bear having anyone know how low I've sunk."

"You never told anyone? Not even Marybeth? You being such old friends and all."

She had a hearty chuckle over that one.

"Yeah, I told Marybeth. And you know what she did? She offered to loan me some money. *At one percent lower than the prevailing bank rate.* Those were her exact words. Here I was at the end of my rope, and she was talking to me like a goddamn loan officer. I wanted to wring her neck, the little shit."

The veins on her neck throbbed in anger.

So those tears at the spa were just an act. Now that she was three sheets to the wind, Ashley's true feelings about Marybeth were coming out.

"Colin told me she left you money in her will," I said. "That has to count for something."

"Ten grand. Big deal. She knew how much I was hurting. She left millions to relatives she hadn't seen in years, and I got ten grand. That'll barely pay the pool man. But I forgot. I don't have a pool man any more, do I?"

She laughed bitterly.

"You want to hear something funny? Back in college, I was the successful one, the one everybody said was going to go places, not Marybeth. She was a nobody. Barely managed to graduate. And you should've seen her back then—before her nose job, and her $500 highlights. You wouldn't have looked at her twice."

She stared down into her empty gin glass.

"But then everything changed. Marybeth was the one who went out and conquered the world. And me? I didn't live up to my promise. All I did was marry well. And then, not so well after all, huh?"

She looked up at me, her eyes hard and bitter. The big-hearted, fun-loving gal I'd known at the PMS Club had vanished. Underneath that happy-go-lucky exterior, Ashley was a very angry woman.

I wanted to tell her that it wasn't too late, that she could still make something of her life, that all she had to do was sober up, and sooner or later she'd find a decent job and maybe even a decent guy. I wanted to tell her all that, but I didn't get a chance, because just then the doorbell rang.

"Get that for me, will ya, hon?" she said. "I got a headache."

I left her lying on the sofa, cradling the bottle of gin in her arms, and answered the door.

A burly guy with a clipboard was standing outside. Behind him I could see a tow truck with the logo "Ace Reliable" emblazoned on its side.

"You Ashley Morgan?" he asked, consulting his clipboard.

"No, I'm afraid she's not feeling very well."

"I'm here to repo her Jag. Either she makes it easy and gives me the key. Or I jimmy the lock and tow it without the key."

"Sorry, pal, I'm not giving you the key." Ashley staggered into the foyer, clutching her bottle of gin. "You're gonna have to work for your money."

Mr. Reliable shrugged. "Doesn't matter to me, lady. I get paid by the hour."

He went over to his tow truck and pulled out a crowbar.

"Screw you!" Ashley shouted out to his beefy back. Then she polished off the last of the gin and slammed the door shut.

"My beautiful Jag," she moaned. "I can't bear to watch."

And while Mr. Reliable went about his business repossessing Ashley's Jaguar, I led her upstairs to her bedroom, barren except for a table lamp and mattress on the floor. I settled her in bed with a cold washcloth on her forehead and then made my way downstairs, just in time to see the silver Jag being towed away.

For the first time I noticed her vanity license plate: RICH B*TCH.

Not anymore, I thought. Not any more.

It wasn't until I was halfway home that I realized the implications of what I'd just seen.

Ashley was in desperate need of money. Maybe she'd known that Marybeth was going to leave her money in her will and just assumed it was a bundle. Maybe she was getting tired of drinking rotgut booze and working nights in a telemarketing boiler room.

And maybe—fueled by anger, jealousy and way too much gin—she decided to go after her inheritance with the help of a little peanut oil.

YOU'VE GOT MAIL

TAMPA TRIBUNE

TAMPA VISTAS RESIDENT RUNS NAKED THROUGH STREETS OF RETIREMENT COMMUNITY

Tampa Vistas resident Hank Austen was apprehended last night running through the streets of Tampa Vistas stark naked, a large rottweiler nipping at his heels.

Witnesses said the dog belonged to the Reverend James Sternmuller, whose home Austen was seen breaking into earlier in the evening.

Mr. Austen was incarcerated for several hours before being released into his wife's custody.

Reverend Sternmuller has agreed not to press charges.

"The poor fellow needs counseling," he said. "Preferably in a locked facility."

To: Jausten
From: Shoptillyoudrop
Subject: Your Daddy, The Ex-Con

Hi, darling—

I've been too miserable to write before now, but I suppose you've got to be told: Your Daddy is an ex-con!

It's true. He was arrested the other night and locked behind bars for three whole hours. And I had to go down to the jail to bail him out. Frankly, I was so disgusted with him, I almost left him there.

You're not going to believe this, but your father broke into Reverend Sternmuller's house to look for Hugo Boss ties!

He broke the window on his back door and busted in while Reverend Sternmuller was at the clubhouse playing bingo. Then he snuck upstairs to his bedroom and searched all his drawers and his closet. Naturally, there were no Hugo Boss ties. In fact, when he looked in the closet, he actually found a carton of bibles! Not to mention a picture of Reverend Sternmuller with Billy Graham. So much for being a killer!

And then, while Daddy was snooping around, he noticed that Reverend Sternmuller had a jacuzzi bathtub. Daddy's been wanting one of those forever. So, not content with merely breaking and entering, Daddy decided to take a bath in Reverend Sternmuller's tub!

"What on earth possessed you to do such an idiotic thing?" I asked him on the way home from jail. He told me he figured Reverend Sternmuller would be away at the bingo game for hours. And as it turns out, he was right. Anyhow, he took his silly bath. Without even bothering to rinse out the tub when he was through!

And then—it just keeps getting worse—he decided he was hungry, so he wrapped one of Reverend Sternmuller's towels around his waist and went downstairs to the kitchen for a snack. Of course there was plenty to eat, because Greta Gustafson has been cooking meals nonstop ever since Reverend Sternmuller moved in. Daddy found a lovely turkey drumstick and just helped himself to it, without a second thought.

So there he was, stealing food from a retired minister, when he wandered into the living room and tripped over a bear skin rug.

Only it turns out it wasn't a rug, but Reverend Sternmuller's deaf rottweiler Brutus! Brutus took one look at this strange man in the house and sprung into action. The next thing Daddy knew, the dog had the bath towel in his massive jaws and ripped it from his waist. Daddy ran for his life, out the front door, Brutus in hot pursuit.

And that's how the cops found your father, running through the streets of Tampa Vistas buck naked!

Of course, Daddy made such a racket busting into Reverend Sternmuller's house, at least five eyewitnesses saw him breaking and entering. Which is why the cops hauled him off to jail. What's worse, the story was picked up by the *Tampa Tribune*, so now, in addition to being the laughingstock of Tampa Vistas, we're the laughingstock of the entire Gulf Coast.

Oh, dear. I think I'll skip the Stress-Less tonight and go straight to the sherry.

XXX
Mom

To: Jausten
From: DaddyO
Subject: Little Mishap

I suppose your mom has told you about my little mishap at Reverend Sternmuller's house. I don't understand how I could have been so wrong about the guy. The Nose is never wrong. But I guess everybody is entitled to a mistake now and then. Your mom is making me write a formal letter of apology.

Your loving,
Daddy

P.S. A word of advice: Stay away from bearskin rugs, especially if they're snoring.

To: Jausten
From: Shoptillyoudrop
Subject: All's Well That Ends Well

You know, darling, I've been thinking it over and I've decided that things aren't so bad, after all. Maybe this whole humiliating escapade will serve as a lesson to Daddy, and teach him to mind his own beeswax! Yes, the more I think about it, the more I'm convinced that everything has worked out for the best.

And speaking of things working out for the best, guess what? Reverend Sternmuller has proposed to Greta Gustafson. Isn't that grand? Wedding bells will be ringing any day now!

That's all for now, honey. I've got to run to the market. For some strange reason, we're all out of sherry.

Chapter 18

"Susie the Slug is pregnant!"

Kandi called me the next morning with the latest bulletin from the set of *Beanie & the Cockroach*. When the phone rang, I was sitting on the edge of the bathtub, trying not to think about Daddy running naked through the streets of Tampa Vistas, and just about to bite into a plump cheese danish I'd picked up for breakfast. I reluctantly abandoned my danish and raced to the living room to answer the phone.

"Can you believe it?" Kandi wailed. "She went into labor last night and was rushed to the hospital."

"Really? I thought slugs just laid eggs."

"Not the character. The actress. Now we have to write her out of the script. Just when we finished writing Ernie the earwig out of last week's script."

I offered her my deepest condolences.

"I am so pissed. Steve and I were supposed to meet Armando to choose a wedding cake this afternoon. Now Steve's going to have to go without me. You know how important this whole cake thing is, don't you?"

"Ranks right up there with nuclear proliferation."

"Seriously, Jaine. They did a survey, and it turns out that the thing people remember most about the wedding is the cake."

"Funny, I always thought it was the full bar."

"Anyhow, I simply had to talk to you, sweetie, what with you being such an expert on desserts."

I didn't know whether to be flattered or insulted at that crack.

"So what do you think? German chocolate with white frosting, or yellow cake with raspberry filling?"

"Kandi, when it comes to a choice between chocolate and anything else, the answer is always chocolate."

"But the raspberry is so pretty," she said.

Only skinny people choose food because it looks pretty. I don't know about you, but I'd eat a dump truck if it was made out of chocolate.

Kandi rambled on for a while about the pros and cons of chocolate versus strawberry. All this wedding cake chat was whetting my appetite. I kept picturing that danish, oozing cheese and slathered with icing, waiting for me at the edge of my tub.

Finally, I managed to get off the phone. I was just about to make a mad dash for the bathroom when the phone rang again. Damn. Why does the phone always ring just when you've got a danish on the tub?

It was Ashley.

"Oh, Jaine. I'm so embarrassed about the way I behaved yesterday. I can't believe those terrible things I said about Marybeth. I don't know what came over me. I may have resented Marybeth a little, but underneath it all, I really did love her."

I wasn't buying a word of it. I saw that look in her eyes when she told me how Marybeth had offered to loan her money at one percent below the prevailing bank rate. Ashley loved Marybeth about as much as she loved the guy who towed away her Jag.

"It was really so sweet of Marybeth to leave me money in her will," Ashley gushed. "I had no idea I was going to inherit anything, of course. What a wonderful surprise."

(Translation: *If you're going to try to pin this murder on me, forget it. I didn't have a motive.*)

I still wasn't buying it. She knew she was going to inherit, all right. What she didn't know was how much. It would've been just like Marybeth to raise Ashley's hopes and tell her she was leaving her a bundle, only to disappoint her from the grave.

But I pretended to believe Ashley's song and dance and made a lot of "I understand" noises. What good would it do to challenge her? I had no proof that she knew about the will. No proof at all.

Her mission accomplished, Ashley bid me a cheery good-bye and hung up, undoubtedly to start in on a fresh bottle of gin.

I, on the other hand, had that danish to demolish. But I hadn't gotten two steps toward the bathroom when I heard Lance banging at my front door.

"Jaine! Let me in!"

I took one last longing look at the bathroom and then opened the front door.

"Isn't it great?" Lance said, bounding into my living room. "I knew all along Colin was innocent!"

"What are you talking about?"

"The news. Haven't you seen it on TV? They just charged Rochelle Meyers with the murder of Marybeth Olson."

Damn.

I raced to the bedroom and turned on the television. Sure enough, there was footage of Rochelle being led into police headquarters, Marty at her side. Marty held her elbow protectively but could not shield her from the shouting reporters. Poor Rochelle. She looked like a rabbit caught in a steel trap.

But Lance was oblivious to Rochelle's plight.

"From the moment I saw Colin," Lance started babbling, "I knew he wasn't a killer. Nobody with eyelashes like his could possibly commit murder. And I happen to be an excellent judge of character."

Yeah, right. This from the guy who once dated a "neuro-surgeon" for three months before he found out he was wanted in three states for check kiting and impersonating a nun.

I sat at the edge of my bed as an on-the-scene reporter droned on about how Rochelle, wealthy Brentwood house-wife and founding member of the PMS Club, would un-doubtedly be released on bail.

This whole thing was crazy. Rochelle couldn't have killed Marybeth. A) She didn't have it in her. And B) If she was going to poison Marybeth, why on earth would she do it in front of a room full of witnesses, with a bowl of guacamole that everyone knew she made?

"And guess what?" Lance was saying. "Colin and I are going out! On a dinner date. To that new sushi place down the street. I hear sushi's a great low-carb aphrodisiac."

The on-screen reporter turned things over to a panel of photogenic legal experts who began discussing Rochelle's fate, and I flipped off the TV in disgust. I had to call Lieutenant Clemmons and fill him in on what I'd discovered about Doris and Ashley—and Colin, too. I didn't care how lush his eye-slashes were; as far as I was concerned, he was still a viable suspect.

"Gotta run," Lance said. "Just stopped by to share the good news. Oh, and thanks for the danish."

"Huh?"

I looked up and saw him standing in my doorway, munch-ing on my danish.

"Lance! I was going to eat that."

"Sorry, Jaine. I saw it on your tub and I couldn't resist."

He popped the last of it down his gullet.

"That was my breakfast!" I wailed.

"I'll bring you something from my place. How about a nice rice cake? Only 30 calories."

"Sounds mighty tempting, but I'll pass."

The first thing I did when Lance left was call Lieutenant

Clemmons. Okay the first I thing I did was curse Lance for eating my danish, but right after that I called Clemmons. I wasn't surprised when he didn't answer his phone. He was probably busy charging Rochelle with murder. I left him an urgent message to call me as soon as possible.

By now I was starving. I was seriously considering taking Lance up on his offer of rice cakes when the phone rang. I grabbed it eagerly.

"Lieutenant Clemmons?"

"No. Andrew Ferguson."

I'm ashamed to say that at the sound of his voice, all thoughts of the murder flew out of my fickle brain.

I just heard the news about Rochelle Meyers's arrest. Which means you're no longer under suspicion. I don't think there'll be any trouble offering you that job now."

"Really?"

My heart soared.

"Yes, it's practically yours. Except for a few formalities, of course."

My heart banked. Beware of formalities.

"That's why I'm calling," he said. "We're having a branch managers' meeting today and I was hoping you could drop by and meet everyone."

"You mean they all have to like me before I get hired?"

"No, not at all," Andrew assured me. "The final decision rests with me and Sam. We just need to see how you interact with the others. I know it's short notice, but do you think you could be here in an hour?"

"Of course!"

"Don't worry, Jaine. I'm sure there won't be any problems."

Gosh, he was sweet, wasn't he?

I hung up and turned to Prozac, who was napping on my keyboard.

"Oh, Prozac, honey! The job is practically mine!"

I raced over and swooped her up in my arms.

Funny, she felt kind of heavy. Was it my imagination, or had she actually gained weight? How could that be, with all the low-cal cat food she'd been eating?

Oh, well. She obviously took after me. I've been on plenty of diets where I've starved myself for a week (okay, for a day), and then stepped on the scale only to find I'd gained a pound. Maybe it was just taking a while for her metabolism to adjust.

But I didn't have time to think about Prozac. I had to get ready for my practically-certain new job at Union National Bank, a prestigious financial institution with assets of more than twelve billion dollars. Of course, its biggest asset, as far as I was concerned, was one Andrew Ferguson.

It took me forever to decide what to wear. I tried on outfit after outfit until my bed looked like the communal dressing room at the Bargain Barn. I finally decided on a classic black Ann Taylor suit. True, I'd bought the suit sometime in the McKinley administration, but classics never go out of style, and with a Talbot's silk blouse and a pair of slingbacks I'd picked up half price at Nordstrom, I managed to achieve the Corporate Writer look I was going for.

On the downside, I'd taken so much time trying on outfits I didn't have time to stop off anywhere for breakfast, so by the time I got to the bank I was starving.

Andrew, Sam and about seven bank managers were already gathered around a conference table when Queen Elizabeth the receptionist showed me into the conference room.

Sam looked ravishing in a designer suit that made my Ann Taylor look like something from a *Hee Haw* rerun. Andrew looked pretty darn ravishing himself, his hair still curled seductively at the nape of his neck.

Sam got up from her seat at the head of the table and introduced me to the bank managers, whose names and faces passed by in a blur. There were a couple of white guys, an Asian, an African American woman, and a Latina. All very corporate. All very buttoned-down. It was a good thing they couldn't see me in my usual elastic-waist sweats.

"I'd like you all to meet Jaine Austen." Sam said, showing me off to the gang.

"No relation," I threw in, with a weak laugh.

"Jaine might be taking over as editor of the Union National *Tattler*."

Might be taking over? I didn't like the sound of that.

"Why don't you grab a seat, Jaine?"

There was only one available seat, at the far end of the table.

I sat down next to the Latina bank manager, who shot me a welcoming smile.

"Help yourself to some coffee." Andrew gestured to a coffeepot on the table. "We had some bagels, but I'm afraid they're all gone."

"That's okay," I lied. "I'm not hungry."

I looked at my Latina neighbor and saw the remains of a bagel and cream cheese on a paper plate at her elbow. I would've killed for that bagel. But something told me that reaching over and gobbling it down would not make the sophisticated impression I was hoping to impart. With a sigh, I poured myself some coffee, which I loaded with sugar, hoping that the sugar rush would get me through the meeting.

I tried to look interested and alert as the others droned on about projections and percentiles and other math stuff I studiously avoided learning in school. But my attention kept wandering. When I wasn't gazing longingly at my neighbor's bagel crumbs, I found myself gazing equally longingly at Andrew Ferguson.

I was in the middle of a delicious daydream involving me and Andrew and a vat of Philadelphia Cream Cheese when I suddenly realized that Sam was talking to me.

"—So I thought you could tell us your ideas for the *Tattler*."

What on earth was she talking about? I hadn't even had a chance to look at the darn thing yet.

"But, Sam," Andrew said, echoing my thoughts, "Jaine hasn't seen the *Tattler* yet."

"Here," she said, sliding a copy of the newsletter down to me at the end of the table. "She can see it now.

"You don't mind giving us your ideas, do you, Jaine? I want to see how you think on your feet."

There was no mistaking the challenge in her eyes. Was she trying to sabotage me? I wondered if she'd seen me staring at Andrew.

"No," I said, with a sickly smile, "I don't mind."

I hurriedly looked at the newsletter, a skimpy four-page affair with routine news of hirings, retirements and promotions. Not exactly Pulitzer material.

"So," Sam said, her arms crossed over her chest. "What would you do with the *Tattler*, Jaine?"

How generous. She'd given me a whole thirteen seconds to think it over.

"Well," I said, putting on my tap shoes and winging it, "how about a column called 'Tattler Tales'? Each month, an employee would tell about an experience dealing with clients. I bet there are all sorts of wonderful stories your people could tell. It might be a nice human interest touch. And maybe the person whose story is chosen could get a free dinner in a nice restaurant. Employees might try harder to accommodate customers, hoping to make it into the newsletter."

"Very good, Jaine!" Andrew beamed.

I was happy to see that several of the bank managers were nodding in approval.

"Hmm," Sam said, with a marked lack of enthusiasm.

Why did I get the feeling she'd been hoping I'd fall flat on my face?

"Any other thoughts?" she asked.

She had to be kidding.

"Well, no," I conceded. "Not right now."

"Then if you'll excuse us, there are a few things I'd like to discuss with the others in private."

Suddenly I felt like a sorority pledge about to be black-balled.

"Better take home a copy of the *Tattler*," she ordered, "so you can think up more ideas."

I grabbed the newsletter, murmured something about what a pleasure it was to have met everybody, and headed out the door, hoping my tush didn't look too tubby as I made my exit.

By this time, it was nearly noon and I was weak with hunger. I hadn't eaten a thing all morning. But before I could think of eating, I simply had to pee. I must've slugged down at least three cups of Union National coffee in that meeting, not to mention the coffee I'd had at home.

I dashed down the corridor into the bathroom and flung myself into a stall. I was glad nobody else was in the room to hear me. Trust me, it was Niagara Falls in there.

What a relief. Now I'd head over to the nearest McDonald's as fast as my Corolla could carry me, and stuff my face with a Quarter Pounder and fries.

I'd just unlatched my stall when I looked up and, much to my surprise, saw a man walking into the bathroom. Good heavens. What was a guy doing in here? Then I looked beyond the sinks and saw a row of urinals. Unless they'd started in-stalling tiny showers in ladies' rooms, I'd run into the men's room by mistake!

I could've sworn the little blue figure on the bathroom door was a woman. But in my haste, I could've been mis-taken.

I quickly darted back into the stall.

Okay, no reason to panic. I'd just wait until the guy was

through and then I'd leave. So I waited. And waited. And waited some more. I wasn't the only one doing an impersonation of Niagara Falls that day. Finally, he finished. But then, just as he was washing his hands, another guy walked in.

They started talking about some idiotic football game, a conversation that lasted twelve minutes. I happen to know this because I timed it. At last, they started to leave, but on their way out, two other guys came in. And so it went. For the next hour and seventeen minutes, I sat on the toilet lid in that damn stall, my knees jammed up in my chin so my high heels wouldn't be visible under the stall door.

The less said about what I heard (and smelled) in that hour and seventeen minutes, the better. I once read that men have a less developed olfactory sense than women. And now I knew why. Self-preservation.

On the plus side, at least I lost my appetite.

Guys came and went, a steady procession of men who'd clearly had massive portions of refried beans for lunch.

At one point, a couple of the branch managers came in and I heard them talking about me.

"How do you like the way Sam ambushed her?" one of them said. "Putting her on the spot like that."

"Yeah, but she came through. That *Tattler Tales* idea was pretty good."

I almost blurted out "Thank you" but managed to contain myself.

Eventually the bathroom emptied out. At long last, I was alone. I unlatched my stall and made a mad dash for freedom.

I flung open the bathroom door and ran smack into a guy who was just about to walk in.

Phooey. Just when I was convinced the coast was clear.

I looked up and nearly fainted.

I hadn't bumped into just anybody. The man I'd practically mowed down was —why do these things *always* happen to me?—Andrew Ferguson.

Damndamndamndamndamndamndamn!

"Jaine!" His speckly hazel eyes were wide with surprise. "What are you doing here?"

Breaking the world record for Time Spent Sitting on a Toilet Bowl.

"Actually," I stammered, "I didn't realize it was the men's room. I thought the little blue person on the door was wearing a dress, but I guess not."

We both looked at the figure on the door. Nope. No dress.

"Maybe you can write this up as a *Tattler Tale*," he said, with a big grin.

He clearly thought this whole thing was a riot.

I, on the other hand, was desperately praying for a hole in the floor to open up and swallow me. This was all too humiliating. I'd just have to salvage whatever remnants of pride I had left and make my exit with as much dignity as possible.

"That would be very amusing, wouldn't it?" I said.

Then I walked away, head held high, shoulders erect, and—as I was about to discover minutes later in the elevator—toilet paper stuck to the heel of my shoe.

Chapter 19

The PMS Murder was back in the headlines the next day: DESPERATE HOUSEWIFE CHARGED WITH HOMICIDE; OUT ON ONE MILLION DOLLARS BAIL.

Underneath the headline in the *L.A. Times* was a photo of Rochelle shielding her face from the camera with her handbag. I recognized her wispy ponytail peeking out from behind the Gucci Gs on her purse. Poor Rochelle. What a miscarriage of justice.

I put in another call to Lieutenant Clemmons. Once more, I got his voice mail. I slammed down the phone in frustration and called back on the central number, where I told the desk sergeant on duty that I absolutely positively had to speak to Clemmons, that it was a matter of life and death.

A few seconds later Clemmons was on the line.

"What the hell do you want?"

Okay, so his exact words were, "How can I help you?"

I took a deep breath and told him everything I'd discovered, how Marybeth had been indirectly responsible for Glen Jenkins's death, how Ashley desperately needed the money from Marybeth's will, and how Colin had been boning up on *Cooking with Peanuts.*

To say that he was unimpressed is putting it mildly. I could practically hear him dozing in the background.

"Thank you for your input," he said, when I was through, "but we feel we have a very solid case against Mrs. Meyers."

"But what about my theories? Aren't you even going to consider them?"

"Rest assured, we'll give your crackpot theories the attention they deserve."

Okay, so he didn't use the word *crackpot*, but he might as well have. I could hear it in his voice.

I hung up and sighed. Clemmons had the case wrapped up tighter than a Beverly Hills facelift. And he wasn't about to take direction from a part-time detective in waist-nipper pantyhose. I only hoped Rochelle had herself a damn good defense attorney.

I was sitting on my sofa, feeling helpless and hopeless and wondering how many calories there were in the seven martini olives I'd had for breakfast, when Pam called.

"I just heard the news about Rochelle," she said. "It's crazy. She didn't kill anybody. The woman is afraid to hang up on telemarketers, for crying out loud."

"Go tell it to the cops. They sure aren't listening to me."

"Isn't there anything we can do?"

"Nothing, short of staging a prison break if she gets convicted."

I guess she could hear the misery in my voice.

"Don't feel bad, Jaine. You tried your best."

"I suppose so," I sighed.

"I feel guilty bringing this up when Rochelle's in so much trouble," she said, "but I've got some good news to share."

"Great," I said. "Lay it on me. I could use some good news."

"That audition I went on? I got the job!"

"That's wonderful."

"It's a fast food commercial for Bucko's, a burger chain in the Southwest. I play a talking ketchup packet. I guess they must've been impressed by my star turn as that eggplant in the vegetable soup commercial. Anyhow, it pays big money, and all the Bucko burgers I can eat."

"Congratulations. We have to celebrate."

"That's why I'm calling. How about lunch this Friday? My treat."

"We're on!"

I was glad Pam landed her dream job. Because it sure didn't look like I was going to get mine. Not after that ghastly men's room episode yesterday. The toilet paper on my shoe was probably the final nail in my employment coffin. I'd be surprised if I ever heard from Andrew Ferguson again.

I did, however, get a call later that morning from one of my regular clients, Seymour Fiedler, of *Fiedler on the Roof* roofing, with a writing assignment for a new sales brochure. Short, pudgy Seymour Fiedler was a far cry from the hunka-licious Andrew, but I accepted the job eagerly, grateful for the distraction—and the paycheck.

I plucked Prozac from where she was napping on my computer keyboard and hunkered down to write about the joys of reroofing. But my heart wasn't in it. I kept thinking about Lieutenant Clemmons and how he'd blown me off. I felt like yanking out that silly cowlick of his, one hair at a time.

Finally, after staring at the same paragraph on Fiedler's No-Leak Warrantee for twenty-five minutes, I gave up and drove over to Rochelle's house.

If the cops wouldn't take me seriously, maybe Rochelle's attorney would.

I drove past the gauntlet of news vans parked in front of Rochelle's house and rang her bell.

"Go away," a woman's voice called out from inside. "We're not talking to the press."

Poor Marty and Rochelle. This was getting to be their theme song.

"Rochelle? Is that you?" It hadn't sounded like her. "It's me. Jaine Austen."

A sweet-faced woman in her seventies opened the door.

"Quick," she said, yanking me into the foyer. "Get inside before those vultures take our picture."

When I was safely inside, she smiled apologetically.

"Sorry to shove you like that, but those newspeople out there are impossible."

She wiped her hands on her sweatpants, leaving a faint trace of flour behind. She must've been busy baking when I showed up. I could smell the heavenly scent of warm chocolate in the air.

"I'm Rochelle's mother, Adele."

I suspected she was Rochelle's mom before she introduced herself. The family resemblance was unmistakable. The same wispy hair. The same caring smile. The same dishtowel slung over her shoulder.

"Rochelle told me all about you. She said you were investigating the case on her behalf."

"That's right."

"That's so kind of you, dear. You're obviously a very caring person. And so much prettier than that dreadful picture of you in the newspaper."

Good Lord. Would I never live down that picture?

"Rochelle's sleeping right now," she said, glancing upstairs, her brow furrowed in concern. "Sedatives. The doctor prescribed them so she could get some rest. It's all been such a nightmare."

"I know," I said, nodding in sympathy. "But I've made a few discoveries that might help Rochelle's case, and I was hoping to give her a progress report. I'm sure her attorney would be interested in what I have to say."

"I'm sure he would, dear."

"Do you happen to know his name?"

"It's Fitzgerald, I think. Or Fitzhugh. It's Fitz-something. Or maybe it's O'Connor. Oh, my. This whole murder thing has got me in such a dither. You'd better talk to Marty."

"Good idea."

"He's at the office. The poor man is going to have to do an awful lot of root canals to pay all those legal bills."

She gave me Marty's office address and I started for the door.

"Wait," she said. "Before you go, why don't you come into the kitchen and have some brownies? They're fresh from the oven."

I took another sniff of that heavenly scent.

"With walnuts and peanut butter chips," she added.

Bet you think I said yes, huh?

Oh, ye of little faith. You'll be proud to learn I didn't waste valuable time eating mega-calorie brownies in Rochelle's kitchen.

No, siree. I ate them in the car on my way over to Marty's office.

It was lunchtime when I showed up at Marty's medical building in Westwood.

It was one of those fancy high-rises with a security desk in the lobby and an overpriced pharmacy where you practically need a cosigner to buy a tube of toothpaste. I rode up in the elevator with an enviably slim nurse carrying a container of peach yogurt and a bottle of Evian water. *Now why can't I eat a slimming lunch like that?* I asked myself, brushing peanut butter brownie crumbs from my sweater.

I got off at Marty's floor and headed down the corridor to his office. With any luck, Marty would be there. If not, I'd wait till he got back from lunch. Surely he'd be able to spare me a few minutes before his first afternoon appointment.

I opened the door to the offices of Martin Meyers, D.D.S.

The place was deserted, except for a busty blonde reception-ist angrily tossing the contents of her desk into a packing car-ton. Her white nurse's uniform was near to bursting at the seams, and her bleached hair was tortured into a towering Barbarella do.

I approached her with caution. She looked highly com-bustible.

"Um. Excuse me. I was wondering if I could see Dr. Meyers on a personal matter."

She looked me up and down.

"Sorry, hon. You're not his type. Drop fifteen pounds, get a boob job, and dye your hair blonde, and you might stand a chance."

I sneaked a peek at her monumental bosoms and wondered if she'd taken her own advice in the breast-enhancement de-partment.

"It's not that kind of personal matter," I said. "Anyhow, I need to talk to him. Is he here?"

"No," she said, yanking her phone from its jack and tossing it into her carton. "The lying cheating turd isn't here."

Nothing like a happy employee to make a favorable im-pression on the public.

"Do you know when he's coming back?"

"Don't know, and don't care."

I watched, amazed, as she began dismantling her computer and stowing the components in her carton. Not to put too fine a point on it, but in some circles, that might be called stealing.

"I gave that bum the best years of my life," she said, hurl-ing her keyboard in the big cardboard box. "And what did I get for it?" She looked up at me, her mascara-rimmed eyes blazing with rage. "Zippo, that's what I got!"

She grabbed a Bose radio and threw it on top of the key-board.

"He promised he'd leave his wife and marry me. And all along he was cheating on me. First with that decorator bitch. And I just found out he was screwing around with that kid in Laguna, too."

She reached for a Waterford vase filled with orchids, emptied the water onto a nearby computer, and added the vase to her pile of stolen booty.

Laguna? My mind started racing. Hadn't Rochelle said something about Marty being down in Laguna the day of the murder?

"What kid in Laguna?" I asked.

"Some bimbo at an art gallery."

Wait a minute. Rochelle said Marty had been buying paintings at an art gallery the day of the murder, that the saleswoman had vouched for him. But if Marty had been having an affair with the saleswoman, she could've been lying to protect him.

What if Marty wasn't in Laguna that day? What if he was back at his house, doctoring a batch of guacamole to get rid of an inconvenient lover?

"Do you happen to know the name of that gallery?" I asked.

"Sure do. I found the bimbo's business card in the glove compartment of Marty's car—along with a pair of crotchless panties."

"Can I have it?"

"Honey, I don't think they'd fit you."

"Not the panties. The business card."

"Help yourself," she said, pointing to her wastepaper basket. "It's in there somewhere."

I spent the next few minutes rummaging through Nurse Medusa's trash. Which was a fairly pukeworthy experience, considering she had the unfortunate habit of tossing her used gum in the garbage unwrapped.

At last I unearthed it.

THE MONTAGUE GALLERY
444 LAGUNA AVENUE
LAGUNA BEACH, CALIFORNIA

CISSY MCDONALD
SALES ASS

Cissy McDonald may or may not have been an ass. That remained to be seen. I just assumed that the card was supposed to have read "sales associate." The "ociate" was covered by a wad of Juicy Fruit.

I wrote down the address of the gallery and headed for the door, just in time to see my buxom friend coming out from what must have been Marty's office—with a flat-screen TV tucked under her arm.

Chapter 20

The first thing you noticed about Cissy McDonald was her hair.

It was shampoo commercial gorgeous, a silken blonde blanket falling nearly to her waist. Of course, if you were a guy, the first thing you'd notice would be her cleavage. That was pretty darn spectacular, too. As were her nonstop legs and to-die-for waistline.

And in the Life Isn't Fair Department, the lucky young woman was also blessed with big blue eyes, a perky little nose and, as I was about to discover, an amazing pair of dimples when she smiled. It was easy to see why Marty had dumped Nurse Medusa for her. It was no contest. And poor Rochelle—with her thinning hair and thickening waist—she didn't stand a chance.

"Hi, there," Cissy chirped as I walked into the gallery, a sleek boutique on Laguna's picturesque main drag. The walls were hung with colorful seascapes and cottage-y scenes, expensive souvenirs of a Laguna Beach vacation. It was the middle of the week, and I was happy to see that she and I were alone in the gallery.

"How may I be of assistance?" she said, flashing me her dimples. They must have netted her a lot of sales. "We have some wonderful new seascapes." She gestured to a wall of pastel watercolors. "Aren't they marvelous?"

You didn't have to be a rocket scientist to figure out that Cissy was no rocket scientist. I could practically see the little valentines dotting her i's as she spoke.

"Cissy McDonald?" I asked.

"That's me," she said, a note of wariness creeping into her voice.

"Detective Austen," I said, in my most officious voice. "L.A.P.D."

I flashed her my driver's license, careful to cover the words *California Driver's License* with my thumb. You'd be amazed at how often people fall for that trick. Especially people with dimples and blond hair down to their waists.

Her blue eyes grew wide with fear.

"What do you want?" she gulped.

"Dr. Meyers confessed everything."

"He did?"

She put her fingers to her lips and began biting her nails. I was happy to see that her fingers were short and stubby, her nails jagged and bitten to the quick. At last. A flaw. There was justice in the world, after all.

"I've come to take a new statement from you," I said.

Her face went pale under her beach bunny tan.

"Oh, geez. Am I going to be arrested for perjury?"

"Not if you tell the truth now."

I rummaged through my purse and took out a pad that I kept there to jot down spur-of-the-minute Toiletmasters ideas.

"First things first," I said, pretending to take notes. "You two were having an affair, right?"

She nodded, blushing.

"I met Dr. Meyers about a month ago when he and his wife were vacationing in Laguna. He bought a really expensive painting and told me I had beautiful teeth. Anyhow, we've been seeing each other ever since."

"He wasn't really here with you the day of the murder, was he?"

"No." She shook her head, gnawing at her nails. "Marty was up in Los Angeles. But he was afraid the police might connect him with the murder if they knew he was in town. So we agreed to pretend he was down here with me all afternoon."

"Did he tell you that he stopped by his house that afternoon?"

"No." She looked shocked. "Did he tell you that?"

"Let's just stick to what he told you, Ms. McDonald."

"He told me he was with Marybeth that afternoon. He'd been trying to break things off with her, but she wouldn't let him go. She said if he didn't divorce Rochelle and marry her, she'd ruin his life. She'd started sending him threatening letters at his office. She said she was going tell everyone that he sexually assaulted his female patients while they were under anesthesia. What a horrible, vile lie!"

I wasn't so sure about that. After what I'd discovered about Marty, I had no trouble picturing him copping a feel from an unconscious patient.

"So he told you he was with Marybeth that day?" I asked.

"Yes. He said he finally managed to get her to accept the fact that he wasn't in love with her any more, and that he was going to marry me."

"Dr. Meyers told you he was going to marry you?"

"As soon as he got a divorce from his wife."

And you were stupid enough to believe him?

Just then the phone rang. Cissy shot me an apologetic look.

"Do you mind if I answer that, officer? The owner of the gallery gets pissy if I don't answer the phone."

"Go right ahead."

She hurried to the phone, her hair rippling in silky waves as she ran.

"Montague Gallery," she squeaked into the phone. "Oh, Marty! I'm so glad it's you." Relief flooded her voice. "The police are here, questioning me."

Uh-oh. This was my cue to exit.

"Yes, a police officer is here right now. What did you say your name was, ma'am?"

"Um. Krupke. Officer Krupke."

Okay, so I panicked and gave her the name of a character from *West Side Story*. Big deal. Don't tell me you never panic under pressure.

"Wait a minute," she said. A light bulb went off over that fabulous head of hair.

"That's not the name you gave me before."

"That's because I'm working undercover. Well, gotta run if I don't want to hit rush hour traffic."

And before you could say Officer Krupke, I was back in my car and headed for the freeway.

It turns out I did get stuck in rush hour traffic. I inched home that afternoon at an agonizing pace. Pedestrians were making better time than I was.

But on the plus side, I had plenty of time to think about what I'd learned that day. Clearly Marty Meyers was the unmitigated rat we'd all thought he was when we first learned of his affair with Marybeth. Can you believe the nerve of that guy? Cheating on Rochelle with Nurse Medusa. Then cheating on N.M. with Marybeth. And then cheating on all three of them with Cissy. The man deserved a gold medal in adultery.

What a fool I'd been to be taken in by his Academy Award–winning performance as The Loving Husband.

And I wasn't the only fool. Poor Cissy. She actually thought Marty was going to marry her. Marty had no intention of marrying Cissy, Nurse Medusa, or anyone else for that matter. Why pay alimony to Rochelle when he could have all the sex he wanted on the side? And if Rochelle went to jail for the murder of Marybeth, then he wouldn't even have to sneak around any more. He could go on non-stop boffathons between jail visits.

Lord knows what he told the cops. Maybe he told them Rochelle was mentally unstable, a nutcase ready to crack. Maybe he didn't come right out and say it, maybe he just implied it, laid in a subtle hint or two that Rochelle was emotionally fragile, on the verge of a breakdown. While pretending to champion her, he could've been planting the seed of suspicion in the cops' minds. Who better to know the mental state of Rochelle than her husband?

And I didn't believe for a minute that he'd broken up with Marybeth on the day of the murder. If that were true, why had she been bragging to the PMS Club about marrying him?

I bet he didn't even try to see her that day. Instead, he decided to get rid of her once and for all—before she had a chance to spread those nasty molestation rumors.

Marty Meyers wasn't in Laguna Beach on the day of the murder. And he wasn't at Marybeth's apartment, either. If I was right, he was in his own kitchen, adding peanut oil to his wife's guacamole.

It was a nifty theory. Too bad I didn't have any evidence to back it up. If only I could prove that Marybeth had been blackmailing him, the cops would have to take him seriously as a murder suspect.

By the time I finally made it off the freeway I was exhausted, emotionally and physically. I wanted nothing more than to go home and soak in the tub till I was limp as a lo mein noodle.

But there was one tiny chore I had to take care of first.

I had to break into Marty's office and search for Marybeth's blackmail letters.

Chapter 21

"Can I help you, miss?"

The night security guard at Marty's medical building looked up from the article he was reading in the *National Enquirer*—a hard-hitting piece of investigative journalism called *I Was the Love Child of Condoleeza Rice and Barney Frank*.

A skinny guy with a bobbing Adam's apple, the guard's name tag read "Chester."

"Hi, Chester," I said, plastering on my perkiest smile. "I'm Dr. Meyers's new receptionist. First day on the job, and I'm working late already. Haha."

I shrugged in mock helplessness, one working stiff to another.

I guess I must have passed muster as a dental receptionist burning the midnight oil, because he pointed to a large ledger on the marble counter and said:

"Just sign in."

"Right," I said, scribbling a fictitious name on the page.

He turned the book around and checked my entry.

"Mildred Pierce?"

I really had to start thinking up original phony names. Lucky for me, Chester wasn't a fan of old Joan Crawford movies.

"Nice to meet you, Millie. Go right ahead."

I started for the elevator, then slapped my forehead, hoping I looked like a person who'd just remembered she'd forgotten the key to her office.

"Darn," I said. "Silly me. I forgot my key." I offered up an apologetic smile. "Would you mind awfully letting me in?"

"Okay, Mil," he sighed, tearing himself from the adventures of Condoleeza and Barney.

We rode up in the elevator together, Chester jingling his keys in time to the Muzak. Outside Marty's office, he took out a master key from his pocket and let me in.

"Be sure to turn off the lights when you leave," he said, flipping them on.

"Of course," I promised. "And thanks so much."

I thought he'd go scooting right back to Barney and Condoleeza. But no, he just stood there watching me. So I walked over to the nurse's station, as if I were really there to do some work. Someone had cleaned up in the wake of Hurricane Medusa, and things were neat, if somewhat devoid of electronic appliances. I took a seat at one of the desks and reached for a pad and pen.

"Thanks again," I said to Chester, flashing him another grin.

"Sure thing," he nodded, and finally walked off, jangling his keys.

The minute he was gone, I made a beeline for Marty's office, which I found at the end of a plushly carpeted hallway. The room was done in sleek teak furniture, very Danish Dental Moderne.

But I wasn't there to check out the décor; I had some serious snooping to do. I hurried over to Marty's desk, which was noticeably free of wifely photos, and started scavenging through his drawers.

I found the usual assortment of paper clips and Post-its, along with a box of *Dr. Martin Meyers, D.D.S.* ballpoint pens. Tucked beneath the Dr. Marty pens were some greeting cards from Cissy. The kinds with kittens on the covers and messages like *You're Purrrfect* inside. I was right about her. She did dot her i's with little valentines.

The bottom right-hand drawer yielded a Beverly Hills Yellow Pages, a box of contraceptive sponges and enough condoms to stock a drugstore. Marty may have been a lying cheating amoral piece of slime, but at least he practiced safe sex.

I sighed, disappointed. So far, plenty of evidence of adultery. But none of blackmail.

Next I checked out Marty's teak credenza, but all that held was a bottle of scotch and a couple of dental textbooks. I rummaged through the pockets of the scrubs in his closet but came up empty-handed.

Then, on an impulse, I sat down on the floor and started rifling through Marty's textbooks. The thick volumes would make a perfect hiding place.

Unfortunately, I didn't find any blackmail letters, but I did find several glossy photos of Nurse Medusa stretched out on Marty's dental chair, naked except for a spit bib.

Just when I was making a mental note to never again sit in a dentist's chair without first disinfecting it, I heard—

"What the hell are you doing here?"

I looked up and saw Marty glowering in the doorway.

I'd been so engrossed in the adventures of Nurse Medusa, I hadn't heard him coming. Damn that carpeting in the hallway. It had obviously muffled his footsteps.

The last time I'd seen Marty, he was a cuddly teddy bear. Now, with his massive shoulders, short neck, and eyes narrowed into angry slits, he looked more like an attacking grizzly. I felt my palms turn clammy with sweat.

"Chester called to tell me my 'new receptionist' showed up," he growled. "It's building policy. The night guards always have to report anyone who shows up without a key."

His stocky body cast an ominous shadow in the room. I wanted to run but was frozen to the spot.

"I figured it was you," he said. "Cissy described 'Officer Krupke' to me and—what a coincidence—she sounded just like you, Jaine. Or should I call you Mildred?"

I finally managed to get to my feet, my knees trembling en route.

"I repeat," he said, his jaws tight with rage. "What the hell are you doing here?"

Then suddenly I thought of poor Rochelle, discarded like a used Kleenex, and I was angry in spite of my terror.

"I'm just trying to save Rochelle's neck."

"You better think about saving your own neck, sweetheart."

And, trust me, there was no affection in the word *sweetheart.*

By now he was a mere arm's length away. Before he could get any farther, I did what I should have done in the first place. I picked up a heavy tome on *Advanced Dental Abscesses* and hurled it at him.

He ducked to miss it. I took advantage of the moment and ran past him out the door as fast as my legs could carry me, which—sad to say—was not fast enough. Somewhere between his office and the reception area, Marty grabbed me by the arm and locked me in a viselike grip. A searing pain shot up my arm.

I looked over at the patient cubicle behind him and saw a drill gleaming in the moonlight. Suddenly all I could think of was the movie *Marathon Man,* where Dustin Hoffman gets tortured by the evil Nazi dentist Laurence Olivier.

My anger had vanished; I was back to being terrified again. I had to do something quickly, before he had me strapped to a chair and begging for mercy.

"You should know," I lied, "that I've told my friends everything about you—about your affairs, about Marybeth's blackmail letters, and about the way you were molesting your patients."

His ruddy face went pale, and I couldn't help noticing that he didn't try to contradict me. There was no outraged, *What are you talking about?*

He'd been molesting those patients, all right.

"Not only that, I wrote everything down and put it in my safe deposit box. If anything should happen to me, I've left instructions with my friends to take that information to the police."

My lie worked. Suddenly Marty's shoulders sagged and he relaxed his grip on my arm. At which point there was a knock on the door, and Chester the guard came strolling in.

"Everything okay, Dr. Meyers?"

Marty smiled stiffly.

"Everything's fine," he said, through gritted teeth. "Just fine."

"I guess I'll be running along now, Dr. Meyers," I said. "The new appointment schedule is on your desk."

He nodded numbly as I headed out the door with Chester.

"You want some advice, Millie?" Chester said, as we rode down in the elevator together. "Watch out for Dr. Meyers. Around here the gals call him Tall, Dark and Hands." He winked conspiratorially. " 'Cause he can't keep his hands off the ladies, if you get my drift."

"I get it, Chester. Believe me, I get it."

And I looked down at my arm, which was already turning black and blue.

I was exhausted when I finally made it home that night. I staggered into my apartment and found Prozac sprawled out on the sofa, in the middle of her umpteenth nap of the day. Lord, how I envied her.

She looked up at me and yawned. I'd expected her to be ravenous. After all, it was hours past her dinnertime. But she pecked at her Lite 'N Lively Liver Snaps like Scarlett O'Hara eating barbeque at Twelve Oaks.

Fiddle dee dee, I get so full so fast nowadays.

Maybe her stomach was shrinking. Mine, however, was as big as ever. I sat on the edge of the tub and practically inhaled the moo shoo pork I'd picked up on the way home.

I was way too tired to take that bath I'd promised myself. I just brushed my teeth—although it was tough even going near a toothbrush after what I'd just been through—and crawled into bed.

I was fairly certain I'd scared off Marty with my threat about the safe deposit box.

But, taking no chances, I drifted off to sleep with my vicious attack cat curled under one arm, and a can of pepper spray under the other.

Chapter 22

There was no doubt in my mind when I woke up the next morning: Marty was the killer.

He'd grown tired of Marybeth, just as he'd tired of Nurse Medusa and Rochelle. And when Marybeth decided to play rough with blackmail, he decided to play rougher with murder.

I called Lieutenant Clemmons and left a message to that effect, telling him how Marybeth had been blackmailing Marty and how Cissy had been lying to give Marty an alibi. Of course, Cissy would certainly deny what she'd told me at the gallery. If only I'd had the foresight to bring along a tape recorder. And without those blackmail letters, Clemmons would never believe me. I could just picture him rolling his eyes as he listened to my message.

As for my original plan—spilling my guts to Rochelle's attorney—that was out of the question. I sincerely doubted Rochelle's attorney would be interested in convicting the guy who was paying his legal fees.

The whole thing was so damn frustrating. Rochelle was about to be tried for a crime she didn't commit. And I was just sitting there with my hands tied.

So I did what I always do when I hit a seemingly insurmountable obstacle.

I put on my running shoes and went out for a brisk jog,

clearing my brain and fortifying myself with energy-producing endorphins.

Okay, so I didn't go out for a jog. I went out for cinnamon buns. The only thing that got fortified was the cellulite in my thighs.

I spent the rest of the day trying to work on the *Fiedler on the Roof* brochure, but once again, I was having trouble concentrating. I couldn't shake the feeling that Marty was out to get me. I kept telling myself that I scared him off with my threat about a damning letter in my safe deposit box. Not that I had an actual safe deposit box. My idea of a safe deposit box was an old sock with $20 stuffed in the toe.

But like I said, I was jittery all day long. Before I got in my car to drive over to my class at Shalom that night, I checked under my tires for nails. I even looked under the hood for a car bomb. (Not that I knew what a car bomb looked like, but I figured if I saw dynamite tied to the fan belt, it probably wasn't a good sign.)

On the ride over my heart leapt at every horn that honked and every car that cut in front of me. And my eyes were constantly darting to the rearview mirror to make sure no one was tailing me.

But thankfully, there were no scary surprises on the road that night.

Nope, the big surprise was waiting for me at Shalom.

Goldie was gone. Vanished. Flown the coop.

There was no sign of Mr. Goldman's sweetheart, the glam'rus gal from Paramus, when I showed up at class that night.

Mr. Goldman sat alone at the conference table, slumped in his chair, unaccustomedly silent. Whatever he'd been using to dye his hair had been washed out, and his feeble excuse for a mustache had bit the dust. Gone was the flashy Romeo in the

THE PMS MURDER   211

loud sports jacket, and in his place was a little old man in baggy corduroys and a stained cardigan.

Mrs. Pechter and the other ladies were chattering among themselves as I took my seat at the head of the table. Was it my imagination, or did they seem particularly chipper tonight?

"Where's Goldie?" I asked, looking around the room.

"She moved!" Mrs. Greenberg announced. "To a retirement home in Las Vegas!"

"Shalom was too boring for her!" Mrs. Rubin chimed in.

"I heard she moved there," Mrs. Pechter said, smirking at Mr. Goldman, "to be near an old boyfriend."

She popped a caramel in her mouth triumphantly.

In the old days Mr. Goldman would have risen to the bait. He would've strenuously denied the boyfriend rumors and insisted that Goldie moved to Vegas for the weather or her health or to be closer to a cherished grandchild. He would've come up with something.

But that night, he just sat there, staring down at the liver spots on his hands. I could practically see him cringing at each verbal dagger.

Normally my sympathies were with the ladies, but tonight, I'd switched allegiances. The gals were showing him no mercy. They chattered on about Goldie's alleged boyfriend, relishing every minute of Mr. Goldman's misery. For once, my heart went out to him.

"Okay," I said, eager to put an end to his torture, "who wants to read first?"

For the first time in the history of the class, Mr. Goldman didn't volunteer to read. He sat there silently all night long, a shell of his former irritating aggravating bombastic self. He had no tales to tell of his life as a carpet salesman, no incendiary commentary on the other essays.

The ladies were in their glory, reading their memoirs of weddings and grandchildren and long-dead relatives, secure in the knowledge that they would not be interrupted by Mr. Goldman's hand waving in the air.

The evening passed uneventfully, with none of the usual Goldman-inspired verbal slugfests. At last, the final essay was read, and the ladies began filing out of the rec room.

"Good night, darling!" Mrs. Pechter called out to me. "I gotta hurry back to my room. There's a movie on TV I want to catch." She practically shouted the name of the movie, for Mr. Goldman's benefit. "*Viva Las Vegas*."

Then she and Mrs. Rubin giggled like teenagers and bustled out of the room.

Poor Mr. Goldman. He just sat in his seat, staring down at his hands, which I now saw were trembling.

"I'm so sorry," I said, sitting down next to him. "I know how much you cared for her."

He looked up at me, with small sad eyes, and shrugged his narrow shoulders.

"It's the story of my life. You may have trouble believing this, Jaine, but I've never been a success with the ladies."

"Really?" I tried to look surprised.

"It's true," he sighed. "Most ladies don't like me. Even my own wife wasn't so crazy about me. You know what her sister said to me at her funeral? That she died in self-defense."

"I'm sure that's not true," I said. "I'm sure your wife died of a real disease."

I patted the liver spots on his hand.

"C'mon, now. Goldie isn't the only woman in the world. Why don't you try one of the other ladies here at Shalom?"

"Believe me, I've tried. They all turned me down. Even that battle-ax Pechter."

I blinked in surprise. I had a hard time picturing Mr. Goldman making a pass at the formidable Mrs. Pechter.

"Face it, Jaine, I'm not a loveable person."

And with that, he started crying. He tried to pretend it was a cough, but I could see tears coming down his cheeks.

"Please, Mr. Goldman. You mustn't cry. I'm sure there's someone out there who'd be happy to do things with you."

"How about you?" he sniffled. "You never want to go out with me."

"That's because I'm young enough to be your grand-daughter."

"So? We don't have to be boyfriend/girlfriend. It can be platonic. Trust me, the porch light is on upstairs, but the fire in the furnace went out a long time ago."

He looked up at me with red-rimmed eyes.

"So how about it?"

He looked so damn sad and vulnerable, I guess I tem-porarily lost my powers of rational thinking. Because the next thing I knew I was saying:

"Okay, I'll go out with you."

The minute the words were out of my mouth, the old Mr. Goldman sprang back to life.

"Okay, cookie. It's a date!"

I was beginning to regret this already.

"Brush up on your mambo!" he said, wiping his tears away with the sleeve of his soup-stained cardigan. "We're going to Mambo Mania."

As they say at Shalom, "Oy."

"Oh, Prozac! You won't believe what I just did."

I tossed my keys on the dining room table and headed for the kitchen.

"I actually agreed to go dancing with Mr. Goldman," I called out as I poured myself a glass of chardonnay. "Was I insane or what?"

I came back out to the living room to tell her about it, but she wasn't stretched out on her usual spot on the sofa.

She was probably in the bedroom, I figured, shedding on my pillow.

"Can you believe it?" I said, heading down the hallway.

"Mambo Mania? With Mr. Goldman? Talk about your dates from hell. It's like going dancing with a Keebler elf."

But when I got to the bedroom, there was no sign of her.

A tiny knot of fear began to form in my stomach.

I told myself to stay calm. She was probably hiding under the bed. But I knew better. Prozac's not a skittish cat. She never hides. I checked under the bed, and under the sofa. In the kitchen and the bathroom. And in every cupboard and closet in the apartment. She was nowhere to be found.

By then, of course, I was crazed with fear.

There was no doubt about it. Prozac was missing.

And I knew who took her: Marty.

All day long I'd had this feeling that he was going to try something. And I was right. Unable to go after me because of my safe deposit box threat, he decided to intimidate me by kidnapping my cat.

I checked the apartment for signs of forced entry. All the windows were locked, just as I'd left them when I went to Shalom. And then I remembered. The bathroom window. I always leave the bathroom window open. There's no ventilation fan in my 1940s bathroom, and if the room doesn't get any air, it's fungus central in there. I'd run around the apartment that afternoon locking my windows, but I hadn't bothered with the one in the bathroom. It was a small window, and I figured no one would be able to squeeze through it.

But I'd obviously been wrong. Marty had somehow managed to maneuver his bulk through the frame.

What a fool I'd been. Why the hell couldn't I have shut the damn window? Wasn't Prozac's life worth a little fungus?

My heart pounding, I raced to the phone and, for the second time in less than a week, called 911.

"I want to report a kidnapping!" I wailed, trying not to think of what Marty might be doing to my beloved kitty with those ghastly dental instruments of his.

A sympathetic operator told me to be calm and took down my name and address.

"How old is the victim?" she asked.

"Seven."

"Male or female?"

"Female."

"Height and weight?"

"About eight inches tall, and sixteen pounds, but she's on a diet and any day now I'm sure she's going to be losing weight."

"Hold on a minute, ma'am. Your little girl is seven years old and weighs only sixteen pounds?"

"She's not my little girl. She's my cat. Someone's stolen my cat!"

"This is the emergency line, ma'am." The kindly voice suddenly sounded a lot less kind. "You need to call the pound."

"No, you don't understand. This is a matter of life and death. My cat has been kidnapped by a murderer. Her life is in jeopardy."

"I'm sorry, ma'am, we don't do cats."

"But someone's taken my Prozac!"

"There's nothing I can do about that, either, ma'am. You'll have to call your doctor for a refill on your prescription."

"You don't understand. I call my cat Prozac."

"And I call mine Mr. Fluffy, but I'm afraid I still can't help you, ma'am."

Suddenly I was furious. Why was I paying taxes if the city couldn't do a simple thing like help me find a kidnapped cat?

"I demand to talk to your supervisor," I shrieked.

"One moment, please," she snapped, and put me on hold.

At which point, there was a knock on the door.

A fresh bolt of fear stabbed me in the gut.

It was probably Marty. He'd hacked poor Prozac to pieces and now he'd come back to get me!

"Can I help you, ma'am?"

A man's voice came on the line.

"Someone's at my front door," I whispered, "and he's going to kill me."

"I don't understand. I thought your cat was kidnapped."

The knocking grew louder.

"Yes, she was. And now the man who took her has come back to murder me!"

Then suddenly I heard: "Jaine, open up. It's me, Lance."

Relief flooded my body.

"Hold on a minute," I said to the operator, and hurried to the door. Indeed it was Lance. And there curled up in his arms was Prozac.

"Prozac!" I cried, grabbing her. "Where have you been?"

Lance handed her over.

"Colin and I were having dinner at that new sushi restaurant down the street, and we found her out back eating from their garbage dumpster."

"What?"

I looked down at Prozac in disbelief. She looked back at me sleepily and yawned.

"Yeah, the chef said she's been eating there all week."

"Prozac, how could you? Pretending to be on a diet, acting all high and mighty and doing your Little Miss Willpower routine, and the whole time you were sneaking out through the bathroom window and stuffing your face with sushi."

"Actually, she was eating the deep-fried tempura when we found her."

Prozac licked her lips.

Yum.

"Why, you sneaky little—"

"I hate to break up this happy reunion," Lance said, "but Colin's waiting. And besides, shouldn't you get back to your phone call?"

I followed his gaze to the phone receiver, which was still dangling off the hook.

Omigod! I'd forgotten all about my call.

At which point, we heard sirens wailing down the street. The 911 operator, taking me at my word that I was about to be murdered, had sent the cops.

Ten minutes later, my face scarlet from nonstop apologies, I slunk back into my apartment, bolted my bathroom window, and poured myself another glass of chardonnay. Then I turned to Prozac, who was stretched out on the living room sofa.

"Well, young lady, having cheated on your diet, scared me half to death and humiliated me in front of the police, what have you got to say for yourself?"

She rolled over and purred lazily.

Got any bacon bits?

YOU'VE GOT MAIL

TAMPA TRIBUNE

PHONY "REVEREND" BUSTED

Legendary drug runner Jimmy "The Rat" Stakowski was arrested by local authorities today for possession of narcotics and misappropriation of funds.

When police raided Stakowski's townhouse in the Tampa Vistas retirement community, where he'd been passing himself off as "The Reverend James Sternmuller," they found a stash of heroin, hidden in hollowed-out Bibles in his bedroom closet. Police also found a check for $50,000 from Mrs. Greta Gustafson, who was under the erroneous impression that Stakowski was going to marry her. In addition to drug running, Stakowski has had a long history of bilking elderly women out of their life savings.

Authorities were tipped off to the presence of Stakowski/Sternmuller by the vigilant efforts of Tampa Vistas resident Hank Austen, who sent fingerprint and DNA samples of the criminal to the FBI.

To: Jausten
From: Shoptillyoudrop
Subject: Can You Believe It?

Can you believe it? It looks like Daddy was right about Reverend Sternmuller—I mean, Jimmy "The Rat" Stakowski—after all. True, he didn't kill anybody. But he *is* a criminal. Imagine. Hiding heroin in his Bibles. Good heavens! When I think of all the casseroles Greta Gustafson cooked for that awful man!

Needless to say, ever since the news broke, Daddy has been lording it over me, reminding me that he was right, and I was wrong. He's so darn puffed up and full of himself. There'll be no living with him now!

I'm just counting the minutes until things settle back down and return to normal.

Your frazzled,
Mom

P.S. That picture Daddy saw of "Billy Graham" wasn't Billy Graham, but Jimmy "The Rat's" bookie.

To: Jausten
From: DaddyO
Subject: Guess Who I Saw?

Hi, honeybun—

Did you see the article from the *Tribune?* About how I practically single-handedly brought Jimmy "The Rat" Stakowski to justice? I knew that guy was fake the minute I saw him. Like I said all along, The Nose knows!

And speaking of The Nose, guess who I just saw at the supermarket, squeezing melons in the produce section? Elvis! True, his hair was dyed blond and he'd lost a ton of weight, but I'm sure it was him. Really. Elvis lives!

Gotta go now and alert the media!

To: Shoptillyoudrop
From: Jausten

Hi, Mom—

Better stock up on sherry.

Love and kisses,
Jaine

Chapter 23

The experts at Merriam-Webster are no doubt debating who should be next to "low-down sneaky scoundrel" in the dictionary: Prozac, or the "Reverend" James Sternmuller.

So Daddy was right to be suspicious of Sternmuller. Who would've dreamed he was really a drug-running con artist? Poor Mom. Daddy would be squawking *I told you so* for months to come. I shuddered to think of him on the hunt for Elvis in the produce section at Safeway.

As for Prozac, I managed to stay angry with her for all of ten minutes. Then she did her rubbing-against-the-ankles-big-green-eyes bit, and I melted like I usually do.

"You win," I told her as I came back from McDonald's the next morning with two Egg McMuffins for breakfast. "No more dieting."

I knew eventually you'd see it my way.

Okay, so I was a pillar of tapioca, a woman who let her 16-pound cat boss her around like a medieval serf. But it was the only sensible thing to do, really. One more day on that diet, and she'd be on Weight Watchers Most Wanted List.

And frankly, I was thrilled not to have to eat another meal perched on the bathtub. How nice it was to have breakfast the civilized way, standing at the kitchen counter, tossing bits of Egg McMuffin to Prozac as she howled at my feet.

As the sunlight streamed in the kitchen window, I felt

ashamed of my crazy call to 911. No doubt about it. I'd gone a little mad. There was no way Marty could have squeezed through my bathroom window.

Nevertheless, all the sunshine in the world couldn't wipe my fears away entirely. Marty may not have broken into my apartment last night, but that didn't mean I'd heard the last of him.

Prozac and I had just polished off the Egg McMuffins and were licking our fingers (well, I was licking my fingers; Prozac was concentrating on her genitals) when the phone rang.

It was Andrew Ferguson. At the sound of his velvety voice, all thoughts of Marty and the murder flew out of my head.

"Good news, Jaine!" he announced. "You've got the job. You're the new editor of the Union National *Tattler*."

"That's wonderful!"

"Can you start tonight?"

"Sure. Your place or mine?"

Okay, so what I really said was, "Absolutely."

"Tonight's the night of our annual dinner dance downtown at the Stratford Hotel, and we want you to cover it for the *Tattler*. Think you can do it?"

Is the Pope Catholic? Is the sky blue? Are fat cells attracted to my thighs like ants to a picnic?

"Of course!" I squealed.

"Terrific. Six o'clock. Stratford Hotel. Formal dress."

After thanking him profusely, I hung up, swooped Prozac in my arms, and danced around the apartment singing *We're in the Money*. That is, until the words "formal dress" registered on my brain. The last time I'd been invited to anything requiring formal dress I'd been a senior in high school, and I seriously doubted I'd be able to fit into my prom dress even if I still owned it, which I didn't.

And so, faster than you can say MasterCard, I was at Nordstrom spending money I didn't have on a fabulous slinky black crepe de chine dress with sexy side slits and sequinned spaghetti straps. With its clean lines and body-slimming cut, I looked practically thin. True, buying it put my checking account into cardiac arrest, but I'd fix that as soon as I got my first Union National paycheck.

Maybe when Andrew saw me in it, he'd forget about all the embarrassing incidents of the past two weeks—my pantyhose on his desk, my face stuffed with burrito, and the ghastly Men's Room Incident. Maybe he'd take one look at me and see only the cool sophisticated writer/editor of his dreams.

I took the escalator down to cosmetics to splurge on some new blush. I was standing there at the MAC counter, dabbing on something called *Plum Foolery,* lost in a fantasy of Andrew and me dancing cheek to cheek at the Stratford Hotel, when suddenly my fantasy came to a screeching halt. Was I hallucinating, or did I just see Marty's face reflected behind me in the make-up mirror? I whirled around and saw a stocky man hurrying out the main entrance. I raced after him, but by the time I got out into the mall courtyard, he was gone.

After last night, I didn't know what to think. Was my imagination in overdrive again? Was that just another big guy on his lunch break?

Or was Marty Meyers stalking me?

I was so discombobulated when I got back in my car, I almost forgot it was Friday, the day of my lunch date with Pam. It's a miracle I didn't get into an accident on the drive over to the restaurant; my eyes were practically glued to the rearview mirror the entire trip. But no one seemed to be tailing me. No one I could see, anyway.

The Farm House is an upscale showbiz hangout in Santa Monica, packed with industry insiders at lunchtime. There are two rooms: an enclosed patio, a leafy sun-drenched haven where the movers and shakers sit. And The Other Room, where the peasants are seated. Don't get me wrong. The Other Room is damn nice; in fact, a lot nicer than the "A" list patio on a hot day when the sun beating down through the skylights makes things a little too sauna-ish for my tastes. And besides, it's light-years nicer than my usual lunch destination, Chez Burger King.

Pam was already seated in The Other Room when I got there, a bottle of champagne chilling at her elbow.

"I ordered some bubbly," she said, wrapping me in a warm hug. "To celebrate my theatrical debut as a talking ketchup packet. Gosh, I can't remember the last time I drank champagne that didn't have a screw-top cap."

"Congratulations, Pam," I said, forcing a smile.

"Hey, something's wrong," she said. "I can tell. What is it?"

And I told her everything. Up to and including my little tête-à-tête with Marty at his office and how I thought he might be stalking me.

"Oh, my God," Pam said when I was through. She poured me a glass of champagne. "Have some. You need it."

She was right. I took a healthy slug of the bubbly.

"You really think Marty killed Marybeth?" she asked, wide-eyed.

"I'm certain of it. If only I could break his alibi and prove he wasn't in Laguna."

"Jaine, this is crazy. You've got to stop your investigation. If you're right about Marty, you could get hurt. I want you to go to the police. Right now. And tell them what you've told me."

"I've already tried. But Lieutenant Clemmons hasn't listened to a word I've said."

"Then you've got to go over his head. See someone else. You could be in serious danger."

"Don't worry. I'm pretty sure I scared Marty off. I made up some story about having a document in my safe deposit box saying that he was responsible if anything happened to me. That seemed to intimidate him."

"Then why was he following you at Nordstrom?"

She had a point there.

"Maybe it wasn't him," I said feebly. "Maybe it was some other big guy."

Pam shot me a dubious look.

"Wait a minute," I said. "Why don't I really do it? Why don't I write down a statement and give it to you? And if anything happens to me, you show it to the cops."

"Okay," she said, as I took a pen from my purse and began writing on a paper cocktail napkin, "but you have to promise me you'll go to the cops soon, *before* anything happens to you."

"I promise," I said, handing her my hastily written document. I only hoped they admitted cocktail napkins as legal evidence in a murder trial.

"You'd better," she said. "Because if you don't, I will. I'll call the cops. I'll call the mayor. I'll call the governor if I have to. I'm very good at that stuff," she said, dipping a hunk of olive bread into a dish of pesto sauce. "I once played a victim's rights advocate in a deodorant commercial."

"Thanks, Pam. I really appreciate it."

"You've got to try this pesto. It's marvelous."

I did. And it was.

It's amazing what a little pesto washed down with a lot of champagne can do for the spirits. I was feeling calmer already.

"Just know that whatever happens, I'm here for you," Pam said. "One hundred percent. You can count on me. Oops," she said, putting down her olive bread and springing up. "Gotta go."

"Where are you going?"

"I see a casting director on the patio whose ass I have to kiss. Sorry, hon. I'll be right back. And then I'll be here for you one hundred percent."

And she scampered off to suck up to her casting director.

I sat back in my chair in a lovely champagne buzz and gazed at the menu, trying to decide between flourless chocolate cake and brownie à la mode for dessert.

Then suddenly someone's cell phone started ringing. I shook my head in annoyance. Why couldn't people shut off their dratted phones so the rest of us could have a little peace and quiet? I looked around to see where the noise was coming from and realized it was coming from our table. It couldn't be my phone, because mine was in the car. It had to be Pam's.

I looked over at her huge leather tote, slung from the back of her chair, and sure enough the ringing was coming from somewhere inside its depths. I reached over to grab it, but in my haste, I knocked it over, sending its contents clattering onto The Farm House's rustic hardwood floor. Quickly I got down on my knees and grabbed the phone, but whoever was calling had hung up.

With an apologetic smile to my dining neighbors, who were staring at me with undisguised disdain, I began picking up Pam's stuff. Good Lord, the woman packed more supplies in her purse than a Nepalese sherpa. It was like a mini-garage sale on that floor. I frantically began grabbing Tampax and mace and movie stubs, a grocery list, a lottery ticket, a Thai take-out menu, a half-eaten jelly donut, a Diet Snapple, a monkey wrench, and a library book due some time in 1987. Just as I was reaching under a neighboring table for an errant package of Rolaids, Pam came back.

"What're you doing down on the floor?"

"Your cell phone was ringing, and when I reached for your purse to answer it, I knocked it over and everything spilled out."

I plopped the Rolaids back into her purse, along with a pair of tweezers. "Haven't you ever heard of less is more?" I hissed.

A snooty blonde handed me a Tootsie Pop that had rolled

under her table. I handed it to Pam, along with her purse and her cell phone, and we sat back down at our table.

"My cell phone!" she said. Her eyes lit up with excitement. "That's the answer!"

"Great," I said, taking a slug of champagne. "Now what's the question?"

"I've got an eyewitness who can prove Marty was in town the day of the murder."

"Who?" Now it was my turn to be excited.

"Me!" she grinned. "I'm an idiot for not remembering sooner, but I bought this cell phone the afternoon of the murder. I got it at Best Buy over in Westwood."

So far, it didn't sound like much of an indictment of Marty.

"And?" I prompted.

"And there's a Ralphs supermarket right next door. When I was coming out of Best Buy, I saw Marty coming out of Ralphs."

"Are you sure it was him?"

"I'm positive."

"He didn't see me, though, and I didn't say hello. I was in a rush, and I didn't want to stop and talk."

"So he couldn't have been down in Laguna that afternoon."

"Nope. He was in town, all right. It must've been about three o'clock. And he was coming out of the supermarket."

"Perhaps with a bottle of peanut oil."

Pam nodded eagerly. "He had plenty of time to sneak back home and doctor the guacamole while Rochelle was preoccupied with the plumbers or the building inspector."

Great. I had an eyewitness who could prove Marty Meyers was in town the day of the murder.

"Will you call the cops and tell them what you told me?"

"The minute I get home," she assured me.

We spent the rest of the afternoon celebrating our new

jobs with an obscenely fattening lunch and another bottle of champagne. I told her about my gala party at the Stratford that night, and she told me about all the things she was going to buy with her residual checks.

We lingered over our flourless chocolate cake and brownie à la mode for hours. By the time we left, the staff was setting up for dinner.

I drove home a happy woman, full of champagne, chocolate, and—most important—hope.

(Okay, most important was chocolate, but hope was a close second.)

By the time I got home, I had less than an hour to get ready for the Union National gala. If I hurried, I could squeeze in a quick soak in the tub.

I whipped out my glamorous new gown from its plastic garment bag and gasped in dismay. After an afternoon in the trunk of my car, it had wrinkled badly.

Oh, well. No problem. I'd just use the steam from my bath to smooth out those pesky creases.

I ran my bath water so it was nice and steamy, adding my favorite strawberry-scented bath oil. Then I hung the dress from the shower curtain rod and dashed to the bedroom to get undressed.

I tossed off my clothes with the carefree abandon of a *Girls Gone Wild* coed. It was finally sinking in that I'd actually landed the job at Union National Bank. Before long I'd be bringing home forty big ones a year! At long last, I'd be able to take my checking account off life support!

True, I hadn't gotten Rochelle off the hook for Marybeth's murder, but it would take months before the case went to trial. I had plenty of time to prove my case against Marty. Pam's testimony would certainly help. In the meanwhile, I had a wonderful new job and an even more wonderful new boss waiting for me.

Yes, I was definitely in a chipper mood when I headed back to the bathroom. A mood that lasted all of two seconds. Because the first thing I saw when I opened the bathroom door was Prozac, perched on the counter, clawing at my new dress.

And then, before my horrified eyes, I saw the sequinned spaghetti straps slip off the hanger. Before I could reach it, the dress went plunging into the hot, strawberry-scented water.

I plucked the sodden mass from the tub and wailed, "Prozac! What have you done?"

Her tail swished proudly.

I just saved us from the evil black monster from the planet Nordstrom!

Okay, no need to panic. I'd simply skip my bath and iron the dress dry.

I dashed to the broom closet for my iron and ironing board. My iron was a rusty old travel model, a treasured anniversary gift from The Blob. The last time I used it was to iron the blouse I wore to our divorce proceedings. I set up the ironing board and began my task. I soon saw that it was hopeless. The dress was soaking wet. It would take hours to iron it dry with my little travel iron. And the one patch I managed to dry puckered miserably under the heat of the steel.

Oh, who was I kidding? There was no way I was going to wear my sexy new dress. Not that night, or ever again. Even if I managed to get it dry, surely it would shrink to the size of a hanky from all that hot water.

And so, with heavy heart, I headed back to the bedroom to look for something appropriate to wear to a formal affair. But all I found in my closet were one-size-fits-all sleep shirts and elastic-waist pants. Which should come as no surprise. After all, my idea of a formal affair is the All You Can Eat Shrimp Festival at Sizzler.

And then I saw it. Way in the back of the closet. My Cinderella-on-Steroids Bridesmaid Dress. I'd picked it up a few days ago from Amy Lee's Bridal Salon and shoved it in back of the closet, hoping maybe the moths would get it. But even the moths wouldn't go near it. I took it out and looked it over. It was every bit as ugly as I remembered. The same puffy sleeves, the same billowing hips, the same hideous bubblegum pink color.

No way was I going to wear this monstrosity. I simply couldn't do it.

Nope. I'd wear my Prada suit, the one I wore to my bank interviews. It wasn't formal, but it would have to do. After all, I told myself, it was Prada. It had style. It had class. And—omigod!—it had a grease stain the size of New Jersey on the front of the jacket. Where the heck did that come from? And then I remembered. It must be from that damn burrito I ate after my lunch with Andrew and Sam.

I would've burst into tears, but I didn't have time to cry. I'd wasted so much time ironing, it was already almost six o'clock! There was no way out of it. I was going to have to wear the cursed bridesmaid dress. I threw on an ancient strapless bra left over from my honeymoon, and my waist-nipper pantyhose.

Then I took a deep breath and put on the dress. Or tried to. The zipper simply refused to budge. Either the dress had shrunk in my closet, or I'd gained weight since the last fitting. Why the heck did Pam and I have to order *both* the flourless chocolate cake *and* the brownie à la mode at lunch? Couldn't we have shared a single dessert like normal women do?

After much grunting and cursing, I managed to jam myself into it. I felt like a sausage about to burst from its casing.

How was I ever going to survive this torture? I'd just have to hope for the best. If I didn't breathe or laugh or eat anything more than a celery stick, I might make it through the night.

I checked my watch. Acck! 6:05. I was supposed to be there five minutes ago! I lassoed my curls into a velvet scrunchy, hoping I could pass off the resulting mess as a sophisticated upswept hairdo. No time to put on my make-up; I'd have to do it in the car.

I grabbed my purse and was halfway out the door when I realized I wasn't wearing any shoes. Damn. I raced back to my closet and put on a pair of Reeboks. What the heck. No one was going to see them under all those mountains of chiffon. The rest of me was in such pain; at least my feet would be comfortable.

Then I headed out into the night in my Cinderella ball gown. Too bad my Fairy Godmother was taking the night off.

Chapter 24

Traffic was a nightmare. Traffic is always a nightmare in L.A. Dinosaurs were probably backed up on the Santa Monica Freeway in the Mesozoic era. Which means I had plenty of time to put on my make-up. Heck, I had enough time to do the make-up for the cast of *Phantom of the Opera*.

Needless to say, my good mood was history.

I looked crummy and felt crummier. What's worse, I'd lost all confidence in my ability to help Rochelle beat her murder rap. What on earth made me think the cops were going to take me seriously? Suddenly I wasn't even sure Marty was the killer. All the facts pointed to him, but something was bothering me. I had this strange feeling that I'd been given a valuable clue that day, but I couldn't put my finger on it.

By the time I got off the freeway, I was already forty-five minutes late. Nothing like getting off to a great start on my first assignment. I seriously considered turning around and going home. But I'd come this far; I might as well see it through.

I checked myself out in my rearview mirror and sighed. No miracle had happened on the ride over. I still looked like crap. I reached for a tissue and blotted my lipstick.

Isn't it strange how little things can be so important? If I hadn't blotted my lipstick, I never would've figured out the truth.

Because when I glanced down at the tissue, that elusive little clue swimming around in my brain came bubbling up to
the surface. At last I knew what had been nagging at me—the
lottery ticket I'd found in Pam's purse at lunch that afternoon. At the time, I'd noticed a red stain on the ticket. I
thought it was the jelly from Pam's donut. But now, looking
down at my tissue, I realized it wasn't a jelly stain I'd seen on
the ticket —but a *lipstick blot.*

I remembered that first meeting of the PMS Club, when
Marybeth held up her winning lottery ticket and kissed it.
She'd left a candy red lipstick blot on the ticket. The same
blot I'd seen on the ticket in Pam's purse.

What, I wondered, *was Pam doing with Marybeth's ticket?*

Suddenly I felt queasy. A horrible thought struck me. Could
Pam have possibly killed Marybeth for the $50,000 lottery
money? Maybe there was no Bucko Burger commercial. Maybe the windfall she was about to receive was from the State
of California. Maybe she stole Marybeth's ticket and then
killed her before Marybeth could figure out what she'd done.

I pulled up to the Stratford and gave my car to a valet.

"You going to the Chang-Germanetti wedding?" he asked,
eyeing my ghastly bridesmaid gown.

"No, the Union National party."

"Really? You're wearing *that* to the Union National party?
Major fashion boo-boo."

Okay, he didn't really say that. He just shrugged and said,
"Rooftop Terrace."

I headed inside and crossed the lobby of the venerable old
hotel, with its original architectural moldings and massive
crystal chandeliers.

Could it be? I thought, as I rang for the elevator. *Was Pam,
my new second-best friend, actually a killer?*

But that was impossible. Pam had been by my side the
night of the murder. She never left me, not for a moment. She
was never alone in the kitchen that night.

But what if Pam was there earlier in the day? Maybe it was Pam—and not Marty—who'd managed to sneak into the house on the afternoon of the murder. Rochelle said that the only people who'd been at the house that day were the plumbers and the building inspector. Could one of them have been Pam in disguise?

Pam was, after all, an actress. She had access to make-up. And Pam was a stocky woman. With a phony beard or mustache, she might easily pass for a guy. Hadn't she been a very convincing man all those years ago in *The Odd Couple?*

Yes, Pam could have been one of the guys at the house that day. And Rochelle, distracted as she was that afternoon, would never have recognized her. She couldn't have been one of the plumbers, though. Surely, they would have noticed a stranger in their midst. But what about the building inspector? What if Pam was the inspector?

When the elevator came, it was empty. The only other passengers who got on with me were an elderly couple and a room service guy with a cart. I wasn't surprised it was so deserted. The Union National employees had probably all shown up ages ago.

The elevator, like the rest of the hotel, was a relic from yesteryear, a spacious cabin with burnished mahogany walls and gleaming brass railings. We pressed the buttons for our respective floors, and the elevator began its slow and stately ascent. At this rate, it would take forever to reach the Rooftop Terrace, but I was already so late for the party, it hardly mattered.

Then suddenly I remembered something Pam had said at lunch today. She'd said Marty probably doctored the guacamole *while Rochelle was preoccupied with the building inspector.* How did she know about the inspector's visit? I'd never mentioned it to her.

No, Pam knew about the building inspector because she *was* the building inspector. While she was upstairs "inspecting" the master bath with Rochelle, she could've easily invented an excuse to check something downstairs and dashed to the kitchen to add a fatal dose of peanut oil to the guacamole.

Oh, God. Pam really *was* the killer.

The trouble with this case all along was that everyone in the PMS Club seemed so nice. No one seemed capable of murder. I knew one of them had to be acting a part. I just never dreamed it was the actress.

The elevator stopped on the fourth flour and the elderly couple got off. The doors slid shut and I was alone with the room service guy. Strange that he was on the guest elevator. Didn't waiters usually ride the service elevators? For the first time I noticed his jacket, and a frisson of fear ran down my spine. If this was the Stratford Hotel, why did his lapel say The Plaza? Was that unnaturally black hair of his actually a wig? And was it my imagination, or was one side of his mustache slightly lower than the other?

Then I looked down at his hands and saw he was wearing something room-service guys rarely wear—nail polish.

"Pam!" I blurted out, before I could stop myself.

"It's me, all right."

There was a manic gleam in her eyes that froze my blood. Gone were all traces of the friendly woman I'd met at the Bargain Barn.

"Too bad you had to drop my purse today. Once you saw the lottery ticket, I knew it was only a matter of time before you figured things out. So I rented this costume and took a chance I'd get you alone in the elevator. Guess I lucked out, huh?"

And with that, she tossed aside the metal cover from the room service tray, to reveal a butcher knife.

Oh, Lord. It was big enough to gut a whale.

Frantic, I sprinted for the control panel to push the alarm

button, but before I could reach it, Pam yanked me back by my ponytail and hurled me against the wall. I howled in pain.

She was stronger than me. A lot stronger.

"Don't be crazy," I said, holding my throbbing head. "The elevator could stop any minute. What if someone sees you?"

"They won't see me. They'll see a deranged room service waiter." She picked up the knife and I felt a wave of bile rise in my throat. "When they find your body, they'll think a man did it. Maybe even Marty. Don't forget. I've got that paper you signed this afternoon blaming him for your murder."

I cursed myself for writing that damn statement. Thanks to my stupidity, Pam was going to get away with murder— twice.

But I couldn't just stand there and let her slice me open like a Benihana chef. I had to keep her talking and somehow get that ghastly knife away from her.

"I don't understand," I said. "Why did you have to kill Marybeth? Couldn't you have just stolen the ticket?"

"She saw me take it from her purse. The bitch had eyes in the back of her head. She threatened to tell everybody. Can you imagine? Telling everyone that I was a thief?"

I refrained from pointing out that's exactly what she was.

"I gave her a sob story about how sorry I was and begged her not to say anything. She said she wouldn't, but I knew that sooner or later she'd blab. And until then, she'd torture me with the threat of exposure every chance she got. She'd enjoy that. And besides, I wanted that fifty grand. You may not mind shopping at the Bargain Barn, honey, but I'm sick of it.

"So you see," she said, her knife poised to attack, "I had no choice. Just like I don't have any choice now. Which is really too bad. I tried to warn you, you know."

"By putting those nails under my tires?"

"I thought for sure that would scare you off. It's a shame

you were so damn persistent. Now I have to kill you. What a pity. I like you, Jaine. We could've been friends."

"Can't we still be friends? I won't tell anyone; I promise. Marybeth deserved to die. You were doing the world a favor. And I'm sure Rochelle's lawyers will get her off on a technicality. Let's forget about this silly murder thing and head on over to Ben & Jerry's."

"You don't really think I'm going to fall for that, do you?"

No, actually I didn't, but it had given me time to inch over to the metal lid she'd tossed on the floor. I grabbed it now and swung it with all my might, knocking the knife from her hands.

As I lunged for the knife, she lunged for me, grabbing me by the train of my bridesmaid dress. I heard the rip of the seams, already *thisclose* to bursting, as they tore apart. Then, just as I was about to grab the knife, I felt a searing pain in my legs as Pam rammed me with the room service cart and sent me sprawling to the floor.

Before I knew it, she was on top of me, frantically searching for the knife, which had disappeared from sight, hidden somewhere under the mountains of chiffon in my dress. At least the dratted dress was good for something. We spent what felt like centuries but was probably only seconds clawing at each other, my dress now completely torn from my body.

By this time I was screaming for help at the top of my lungs. Where the hell were all the people in this hotel anyway? Couldn't anybody hear me?

Then, to my horror, I saw Pam retrieve the knife from under a pile of chiffon.

"Sorry, Jaine," she said, holding it aloft. "Oh, and by the way, thanks again for the resume."

Then, just as she was about to plunge the knife into my chest, the elevator door dinged open, and we were on the rooftop terrace, surrounded by a crowd of gaping Union

National employees. Thank heavens. Someone *had* heard me.

The next thing I knew, a couple of security guards were prying Pam off me and hauling her away. And then the hunkalicious Andrew Ferguson stepped out of the crowd and kneeled down next to me.

"I've heard of bad room service," he said, "but that was ridiculous. Are you okay?"

Was I okay?? Of course I wasn't okay!! I was lying there in front of half the staff of Union National Bank, practically naked in my waist-nipper pantyhose and Reeboks!

"Yes," I managed to say. "I'm okay."

He glanced down at my waist nippers and whispered: "You know, ever since I saw those pantyhose on my desk, I've been wondering what you looked like in them. And out of them."

Then he smiled a smile that made me blush right down to my Reeboks.

What do you know? Looks like my Fairy Godmother was working that night, after all.

Epilogue

Needless to say, the cops released Rochelle and arrested Pam. Her lawyer's going to have one hell of a time explaining the "building inspector" costume the cops found in her apartment.

After all that happened, it was no surprise that the PMS Club broke up. Not long ago, we met for lunch and caught up on the events in each other's lives.

You'll be happy to learn that Doris is engaged to a widower she met at a "How to Survive the Loss of a Love" support group.

Ashley is no longer pretending to be rich and seems a lot more at peace with herself. She's renting out her house to movie production companies and got herself a job as a personal shopper at Saks. Last I heard, she was dating a guy in ladies lingerie. (No, not a cross-dresser, but a buyer from the New York office.)

Colin landed a terrific gig as a personal assistant with one of L.A.'s hottest new caterers. And you'll never guess who that caterer is. Rochelle! Yep, she divorced her ratfink of a husband and went into business doing what she does best—cooking.

After catering some movie shoots at Ashley's house, the word spread, and now Rochelle is whipping up empanadas and margaritas for Hollywood's "A List." (One thing she refuses to make, though, is guacamole. If a customer insists on it, she buys it at the market.)

Marty Meyers is living with his latest mistress—not poor Cissy, but the 19-year-old bimbette he hired to replace Nurse Medusa. Pam was lying about seeing him on the day of the murder. At the time Pam claimed to have seen him outside Ralphs supermarket, he was actually holed up in his office, drilling his bimbette.

Colin and Lance were a hot and heavy item for a couple of months, until Lance let Colin redecorate his living room. I warned him not to do it, but did he listen? Nooo. They got into a huge fight over the coffin Colin expected Lance to use as a coffee table, and things went pffft from there.

Bad news about Kandi. She's single again. Steve dumped her. It seems he fell in love with Armando, the wedding planner. I guess they bonded all those nights when Kandi was working late. At first, she was devastated, but you know Kandi. A month later, she was signing up for a course in Singles Kickboxing.

As for me, I spent six weeks with my leg in a cast. Not from my elevator encounter with Pam, but from tripping over one of Mr. Goldman's two left feet at Mambo Mania. What a night. Trust me, you don't want to know the details. Let's just say it's the last time I'll ever go dancing with a man who uses his dentures as castanets.

My big job at Union National? It was heavenly while it lasted, which was all of two weeks. Yes, two weeks after I started editing the *Tattler*, Union National was bought out by a German conglomerate. One of the first things they did was save $40,000 a year by firing me and folding the *Tattler*.

The second thing they did was transfer Andrew Ferguson to Stuttgart, Germany. A quatrillion miles away. Can you believe it? I didn't even get a chance to go out with the guy. By the time the doctor finally took the cast off my leg, Andrew was *auf wiedersein,* gone with the wind. He called before he left, though, and promised to keep in touch. I'll let you know if he does.

Well, gotta go. Prozac's howling for her dinner.

Catch you next time.

P.S. By the way, I finally got Prozac to stop eating bacon bits. I convinced her that, with all those chemicals and artificial ingredients, they were way too unhealthy.

Now she insists on real bacon.